Dancing With Ana

Nicole Barker

Nicole Barker

The Golden Road Press LLC.
Boca Raton, Fl

Published in the United States of America by The Golden Road Press
LLC. Boca Raton, FL

www.thegoldenroadpress.com

Copyright © 2009 by Nicole Barker
Dancing With Ana cover artwork copyright © The Golden Road Press
LLC. Boca Raton, FL.

For more information or to order this book online, visit
www.dancingwithana.com

Library of Congress Control Number: 2009926841

ISBN 978-0-615-28852-9

"I wanted to keep reading from the minute I read the first line!"
Nicole Caporusso, age 12

"I just kept wanting to know what was going to happen next…I was actually kind of sad when I finished it because I wanted more."
Madison Mirandi, age 15

"I totally got it…..it's really good."
Gabby Perretta, age 13

"It makes you want to keep reading, it had you understand what us teens go through…"
Abigail Zaratin, age 14

"I stayed up all night finishing it, and I didn't want it to end!"
Gabrielle Redding, age 12

This book is the result of the influence of the women in my life.
To my mother, the strongest and most beautiful woman I know. Thank you for your constant love and support. You are always there, and I am blessed.
The grandmothers, aunts and cousins who helped raise me.
My mother-in-law, for her encouragement and support.
The best friends who were a part of the special, yet sometimes tumultuous days of elementary and middle school. The girlfriends who shared in high school adventures and antics with me. The young women who became my sisters during the college years.
And the amazing women I've befriended in the many years since.
Thank You.
If it wasn't for all of you, I would not know the unique experiences that girls and women share. I wouldn't understand the laughter, the tears, the anger, the celebration. I wouldn't know the infinite support, the cheers, the joy. I would never have known the beauty of a friend's love.
I wouldn't be me.
On a more specific note:
I want to thank my "Fab Five": Nicole Caporusso, Madison Mirandi, Gabby Perretta, Gabrielle Redding and Abigail Zaratin. Thank you so much for your valued time and opinions. Their mothers also deserve a mention...Marianne, Susan, Tara, Susan and Pamela...thank you for trusting me with your girls.
A special thank you to Tara Perretta for her ability to look at every comma.
A shout out goes to Kirsten Maurizi for her help with the texting...and to her mother, Chaundra, for everything else.
To my son Nathan: Thank you for your kind and generous spirit, your loving nature, your integrity. You have surpassed any dreams I had of who my son would be, and I struggle to find the words to express my pride.
I Love You.
To my daughter Kaya Rose: You burst into my world and have been in fifth gear ever since. Your strength, quick wit, sense of humor and hell-bent determination in all things takes my breath away in admiration. You are already the woman I've always wanted to be. I Love You.

When it comes to the man I've shared my life with since the age of 22, there truly aren't enough words, nor will there ever be, so I'll simply say.....

for Brian

One

"Christine McCady's hair is especially shiny today," Jenny told the three girls sitting with her at the lunch table. They had known each other since kindergarten, spending countless hours at each other's houses playing with Barbies when they were little, and obsessing over teen crushes as tweens. Now that they were sixteen, their discussions mainly focused on boys and fashion. Their communication was unique, sometimes only requiring a single word, or a look. They were tight, and nothing had ever come between them.

At Jenny's comment, their heads turned in unison to assess the most popular girl in school's glorious mane of blond hair. They turned back around, once again feeling defeated by the unfairness of it all.

"I wonder what she uses. What's the name of that shampoo that's really expensive, you know, the one that's organic?" Melanie asked her friends.

"Whatever it is, you obviously don't need it Mel," Jenny said, glancing at her friend's mane of beautiful, thick black hair that was a result of the combination of her mother's African-American roots and her father's Irish heritage. "Anyway, I don't think it's shampoo. It's got to be something she eats. Whatever it is, it's just not fair. Not only is she dating the hottest guy in school, but she's super rich and beautiful. How can God let one girl have all of that?" she lamented, throwing her French fry down onto her tray.

"She's also thin as hell," Rachel mumbled, her pale blue eyes glancing at Christine's lithe form.

Beth, who had continued to observe Christine throughout the discussion, looked at her friends and said quietly, "I heard she's anorexic, so it can't be anything she eats."

The other girls turned back to look at their school's icon of perfection. She was definitely thin, probably a size two, yet she had full breasts. Her blond hair was thick and long, her skin was clear and the blue of her eyes was almost piercing. She was as close to perfection as they had ever seen in real life.

"See, she's not eating," Beth pointed out to her friends.

They watched as Christine laughed at something her boyfriend, Matt Springer, whispered in her ear. As he turned his attention back to his food, Christine continued to talk to her friends, sipping daintily from a straw in her water bottle. It seemed she was moving in slow motion, every movement full of grace. She commanded the attention of the occupants at her table, reigning over them. Her outfit might as well have come right off a fashion mag, and fit her trim figure like a glove. She was the closest thing to celebrity in their lives.

"…..what's up?" a male voice said loudly behind them. The girls jumped, causing Melanie to drop her sandwich on the floor.

"Shoot! Look what you made me do Jeremy!" she scolded over her shoulder, bending down to retrieve her lunch.

Jeremy, who had been standing by the girls' table trying to get their attention, glanced at Melanie and offered a mumbled apology with a half smile. Then he turned his full attention to Beth. "What's up?" he repeated, looking directly at her.

She smiled up at him. Jeremy had lived across the street from her since they were babies, acting as her constant playmate, eternal confidant and big brother all in one. Over the summer he had grown three inches, bringing him to an impressive six feet-two inches. His body had changed as well, looking more like a young man's body than a boy's. That, combined with his thick head of dark hair and soft green eyes, had captured the attention of many girls this year. All except her friends, who still regarded him as the boy they had been forced to include in their games throughout childhood.

"Oh, we're just observing the alphas eating lunch," Beth responded, scooting over so Jeremy could join them.

"Or not eating," Rachel mumbled, still staring at Christine.

He followed the direction of her gaze and smiled knowingly. There was no doubt Christine McCady was gorgeous. Jeremy himself had found satisfaction on many nights fantasizing about her. But she had always stayed exactly that, a fantasy.

The reality he wanted was sitting next to him. He shifted his gaze slightly so it focused on Beth. Jeremy's appearance wasn't the only thing that had changed over the summer; his feelings for Beth had changed too. One day she was his best friend, the next day he found himself transfixed, halted in the act of getting the mail for his mom. She had been washing her car in the driveway, wearing denim cut-offs and a tight Grateful Dead t-shirt. For the first time, he noticed that she had a nice butt. She'd leaned up on her toes, trying to reach the other side of the front windshield, and offered him a full view of her legs. Even though Beth was only five feet-four inches, she had nice legs that were tight from running and surfing. Her brown hair had been pulled into a high ponytail. It swayed back and forth while she scrubbed her car, an apple red sixty-five Mustang that was her pride and joy.

When she turned to soak the sponge in the bucket by her feet, she caught sight of him. She pushed a strand of hair out of her face with her arm and yelled, "How's it goin'?"

Jeremy, whose mouth had been partway open, had to swallow a couple times before he weakly croaked out, "Good."

He finished getting the mail and slowly walked back into his house, trying to process what had just happened to him. He hadn't been able to get her off his mind since.

"Do you think she's pretty Jeremy?" Jenny asked, her crystal green eyes pinning him with the question.

Now it was Jeremy's turn to jump. He looked at Jenny blankly and asked, "Who?"

"Christine McCady, you idiot, you know, the person we've been talking about the entire time!" Jenny said more loudly than she intended. Quickly, she looked around to see if anyone had heard, but the noise of the lunchroom had muffled her outburst. Breathing a sigh of relief, she turned back to Jeremy, impatiently shoving her dark blonde hair behind her shoulder and repeated, more quietly this time, "Do you think Christine McCady is pretty?"

Four pairs of eyes stared at him expectantly, and he realized that the answer to this question was of the utmost importance. He looked back at Christine, who was drinking water and talking to another girl, and replied, "Yeah, she's pretty, but in an untouchable sort of way." He turned back to them. "Does that make sense?" he asked, hoping the matter was settled.

"Yeah, that makes sense," Jenny mumbled, while the other girls stared at their trays of food.

He got the sense they didn't like his answer at all, but had no idea how to fix it, so he decided to change the subject. "Hey Beth, wanna hit the beach after school?"

She turned to him, smiling, and his stomach felt funny. "Yeah, okay, but I can only go for an hour. I've got tons of homework."

The bell rang and the girls quickly got up to throw away the food on their trays.

"Hey, you didn't finish your lunch," he said as they walked away, but the noise drowned him out.

"What was all that about Christine today?"

Beth glanced up at Jeremy as she secured the leash on her ankle. "Nothing," she said straightening and shielding her eyes from the sun with her hand. "We just wanted your opinion, you know, as a guy."

He stared at her, feeling like she wasn't telling him the whole truth. He knew her better than she knew herself at times. He had an uneasy feeling as he watched her grab her surfboard and head into the water.

"Come on!" she yelled to him.

He shrugged it off, grabbed his board and paddled out to join her. They surfed for almost an hour, catching waves, paddling out again and again.

By the time they headed in, Beth was starving. The fact that she'd only eaten a few bites at lunch and skipped her afternoon snack was starting to hit her. She wasn't used to going without food for any length of time. She used to love eating, and loved food. Before her parent's divorce last year, going out to dinner had been one of her favorite things. Her love of eating out had dwindled significantly over the last year, as did her appreciation of good food. It seemed lately she ate more for sustenance than enjoyment.

She'd also taken notice that the other kids at school flocked around the super thin girls like buzzing bees, hanging on their every word. It seemed all the popular girls were super thin. She'd heard they were anorexic, maybe even bulimic, which had grossed her out. She never could imagine starving herself on purpose. But maybe losing a few pounds would lift her spirits a bit. Anyway, she was always looking for a distraction.

"Wanna grab a smoothie?" Jeremy asked, drying off.

Transfixed, Beth watched him move the towel over his body. Her eyes glided up the length of him, over his chest, past his lips, to green eyes staring back at her. He was looking at her in a way she'd never seen before, and it made her warm inside... everywhere. She was sure she was blushing!

She shook herself out of the trance and said breathlessly, "No, thanks, homework." Grabbing her board, she headed back to her car.

Jeremy stood there, watching her running away from him. A slow smile spread across his face.

Two

"Beth, come down for dinner."

"Okay Mom," Beth yelled back. She wrote the last two sentences on a report that should have only taken thirty minutes, but due to her increased headache, had taken over an hour. Grabbing it off the printer, she put it in her backpack and headed downstairs. The smell of food instantly made her mouth water, and she swallowed it down.

"Grab the napkins honey," her mom told her as she entered the kitchen.

Beth's stomach growled in earnest while an anxious feeling overtook her. She got a bottle of water out of the fridge and sat down at the table. Her little brother, Billy, was already tearing into a piece of chicken while simultaneously shoving rice into his mouth. That sight alone was almost enough to curb her appetite, almost. She turned her attention to the bounty before her, and gave a loud sigh.

"What's wrong honey?" her mom asked, looking concerned. "Is something bothering you?"

She shook her head and began to carefully dish up food onto her plate. Nothing got past Mary Baxter when it came to her kids. In the back of her mind Beth knew she would have to be very careful while dieting or her mom would know within days what was up. She chose a scoop of rice, a couple broccoli stems and a small piece of chicken. She ate it so fast that she got the hiccups.

"Beth, slow down, you're going to choke!" Mary said, laughing. "Is that all you're having?"

Damn, she thought to herself. It was going to be nearly impossible to pull this off under her mother's watchful eye.

"Yeah, Jeremy and I ate after surfing today and I'm still full from that." Out of the corner of her eye she watched her mom accept this explanation.

"Okay, but next time don't spoil your appetite for dinner, okay hon?" she asked with a smile, and Beth knew a moment of guilt.

She never lied to her mom, but was certain that a lot of the decisions she was going to make over the next few weeks would involve dishonesty. As usual, her eyes wandered over to the empty chair that was once her father's.

"Can I be excused?"

"Of course," Mary said, again smiling at her.

Beth quickly averted her eyes, cleared her place and headed back to her room.

She was in the process of writing an email to her dad when she heard her phone, alerting her to a text. She grabbed it off her desk.

"How was surfin with Jeremyyyyy?" Jenny wrote.

"The waves were pretty good" she wrote back.

"You know what I mean B! ;)"

"No..uhm..I don't..srry :/" Beth wrote, although, in the back of her mind, she kind of did.

"Come on B..as much as I HATE to admit it..your little Jeremy has turned out to be QUITE the hottie. And if I'm not mistaken..he's so totally into you!"

"What?!?! No he's not!" Beth wrote, but deep down inside, that warm sensation started again.

Thinking about Jeremy in "that way" seemed impossible, but that was exactly what she'd been doing lately. Something about him had changed, and it wasn't just his looks. There was a new maturity about him, he was almost sexy. The thought that he may feel the same way about her made her feel excited and unsure at the same time.

"Uh...yeah he is Beth. Trust me! I've seen the way he's been lookin at ya lately. The question isn't whether he has feelings for you! It's do youuu have feelings for hiiim?!?"

"I...I don't know what I feel for him Jen. I just don't. He's been my BEST friend for soooo long. It's all pretty confusing..." Beth admitted.

"I know..it's cool. You'll figure it out." Jenny wrote.

"Yeah anyway...totally different subject! I've decided to diet. I want to lose like 10 lbs! :)"

"Ooo samess. I need to lose some weight. We can do it together! :)"

"Cool..we can support each other. I want to lose quickly though..so I'm reallyyy restricting my food. I want to eat under 1000 cals a day."

"Wow..that's not a lot of food. We will totally lose! When should we start?" Jenny wrote.

"I started today...I didn't eat anything except breakfast this morning..a small amount of my lunch and a little bit of dinner. I was really hungry after surfing..and I got a headache..but I feel better since eating some dinner."

"Oh! I'm going to be a day behind you! Oh kay..well I'm gonna eat hardly anything tomorrow. What should we eat for breakfast?"

Beth thought about the food downstairs in her kitchen. "How bout a grapefruit..do you have any grapefruits?"

"No..only oranges. I'll have an orange..you have a grapefruit...Kk?"

"Kk..oh..and water! Drink a bottle of water with it. Then we'll feel full. We'll buy more water at school."

"Cool! I'm so excitedd! Night Bethh!"

"Night" Beth wrote, putting her phone back down.

She turned her attention back to the email, and sighed. Two days ago, at the last minute, her dad had canceled his scheduled visit with them. They had waited over an hour for him to pick them up. He had called just as Beth was starting to worry and told them a sudden business meeting had come up. She knew he was lying, but said nothing, not wanting to upset her brother. Her mother had known it too, but also said nothing, not wanting to upset her children. Beth had gone for a long run that day.

She filled her dad in on the usual stuff..homework, surfing, Billy's football..then got to the point. "What are we doing this Sunday when you pick us up?" she wrote. She couldn't be more direct than that! Satisfied, she hit send and went to bed.

Three

The sounds of the rainforest swirled in Beth's head the next morning. They progressively got louder and louder. She rolled over, hit the button on her alarm clock, and sat up. Her stomach was churning a bit, but she didn't want to drink any water until she weighed herself. This would be her first weigh-in, and she wanted it to be accurate.

She tiptoed into the bathroom across the hall from her bedroom and shut the door. The scale was buried under a curling iron, a big box of tampons and a basket full of suntan lotion. Pulling it out, she wiped it off and set it in the middle of the floor. Taking a deep breath, she stepped onto the scale. 120 pounds reflected back at her. Not having anything to compare it to, she wasn't sure how she felt about that number. She decided to research stats tonight so she could figure out her goal weight.

"Beth, are you in the shower?" Mary asked from behind the door.

"I'm getting in Mom," Beth answered as she shoved the scale back under the counter.

"That's what you're eating for breakfast? That's disgusting!" Billy exclaimed with a very dramatic look on his face. He then shoved a big spoonful of Rice Krispies into his mouth and proceeded to watch her eat the grapefruit.

"Grapefruits are very good for you Billy. I'm eating healthy," she informed him with a sniff. He continued to look at her like she was nuts, then turned his attention to the cartoons blaring from the TV in the family room.

"Grapefruit is healthy, but you should have something else with it Beth," her mom told her as she breezed into the kitchen to pour coffee into a travel mug. "Have some toast too, okay dear?"

"Okay Mom, have a good day at work," she said, watching her mother leave. It was already getting easier to tell little white lies, she thought to herself with relief, and guilt.

"Aren't ya gonna have your toast, like mom said?" Billy asked suspiciously, his big blue eyes watching as she put her dish in the sink.

Beth turned to him, surprised to find an almost maternal look on his face. She attributed it to the fact that he looked exactly like their mother, from the top of his blond curls to the dimple in his chin.

"There isn't time. C'mon, let's go. We still need to pick up Jenny."

"So, did you weigh yourself?" Beth asked Jenny after they dropped Billy off.

"Yeah, I weigh 130 pounds. Is that bad? It sounds bad," Jenny replied.

"I don't know. I'm going do some research tonight. How tall are you?"

"I'm the same height as my mom, five feet two inches. I wish I was as tall as Christine!"

"I know. I'd love to know how much she weighs!"

"Yeah...hey, what are we doing about lunch?" Jenny asked.

"We have to check out the choices today. Remember to keep drinking water. I'm going to go surfing again for exercise."

"I should go for a run after school."

"I'll run with you, then go surfing," Beth said, deciding that the more calories she burned, the better.

As always, Rachel and Melanie were waiting for them in the parking lot when they got to school.

"Hey!" Melanie exclaimed. Rachel waved, but seemed distracted.

Beth walked up to her and said, "What's goin on?"

Rachel pushed her black hair behind her ear, glancing at Beth. She nodded toward a group of kids. "Look at them, they're all so freakin perfect, it drives me crazy!"

Beth glanced over at the group. Christine was in the middle, as usual. They were all laughing and teasing each other. It was like watching an exclusive club to which you would never belong.

"I know, it sucks. Hey, listen, Jenny and I started dieting to lose like ten pounds. You wanna do it with us? It could perk us up."

Rachel turned her attention back to Beth. "Yeah, I'm in. Why not? I need something to focus on."

Beth put her arm around her. Out of all of them, Rachel had the toughest time. Her dad had left when she was two, and her mom lived more like a teenager than Rachel did. Where Rachel rarely had a boyfriend, her mom had a regular string of them. There were many nights she slept over at

Beth's house, just to escape the chaos her mother had created.

"I'm in too!" Melanie said. "That way I can keep an eye on you girls!" From the time they were six, Melanie had always been the mother hen of the group. "Speaking of, the bell's about to ring!" she said over her shoulder, and they followed her into school.

"Need help?" a familiar voice asked. Jeremy plopped down next to Beth as she waxed her board.

"No, I got it. What are you doing here?"

"Surfing, of course!" he said, smiling. He hadn't seen her since yesterday. He'd looked for her at lunch, but neither she nor the other girls had been in the cafeteria. "Where were you at lunch today?"

Beth focused on waxing her board. She had never lied to Jeremy, in fact, she had always told him her deepest, darkest secrets. The thought of lying to him almost made her feel sick. "We ate fast and went outside to hang out. It was such a nice day."

Jeremy watched her hands moving across the board, then studied her face. She was definitely hiding something, which was beginning to worry him. He'd only been five minutes late to lunch after finishing something in the computer lab. Running to the cafeteria to spend time with her, he entered breathless. After scanning the room, he asked a few people if they'd seen her, or the other three girls. No one had.

Beth knew he was suspicious of something. She couldn't tell him, he would never understand her need to lose this weight. Once she made the decision to lose it, she became completely determined to do so. She wasn't even sure why. Jeremy would never agree to her methods. She knew him well enough to know that he would think she was crazy to semi starve herself. She just wanted to feel different, to feel special.

She was also beginning to realize what a challenge it was to not eat, how much strength it took. Beth was never one to walk away from something because it was difficult, and she wanted to prove to herself that she could do it. If Christine McCady could exert such extreme self-control, then she sure as hell should be able to!

He stared at her rubbing the wax onto her board over and over in the same exact spot. Reaching out, he stilled her hands with his. She hadn't realized what she'd been doing. Her muscles were tense, and she was breathing quickly. She stared at Jeremy's hand over hers, feeling the warmth of him. It served as a balm, relaxing her muscles and returning her breathing to normal. She raised her eyes to his, and found him staring intently at her.

"What is it?" he asked, concern radiating off of him.

She wanted to tell him, wanted to explain her need to focus on something...anything. The words were near bursting out of her. How could she explain her desire to try to obtain something that seemed so out of reach? She was afraid he would judge her, because he knew she had always been a fairly secure person. How could she explain it to him, when she didn't even understand it herself? Somehow, the ten pounds she wanted to lose had already begun to take over her mind a bit. She had tried to find something to eat in the lunch line, but it was all too fattening. Finally the four of them had agreed that they would each get a granola bar and water, which they took outside to eat. It was all starting to sound a little crazy to her, so she couldn't imagine what he would think. As she stared into his eyes, she now knew exactly how she felt about Jeremy, and what he thought of her mattered. It mattered very much.

"I'm fine, really," she said shakily. When he continued to stare at her doubtfully, she exclaimed, "Jeremy, I'm fine! I'm just a little stressed with all of the tests and my homework load this year."

She realized that his hand was still on hers, and the feeling was starting to cause some wonderful stirrings. She pulled her hands away and quickly stood up, only to have a sudden burst of dizziness assail her. Jeremy, who had stood up with her, watched her lean forward, then roll back on her heels. He caught her and held tight, afraid she was about to faint. Her head snapped back, and suddenly they were face to face, body to body.

Ever so slowly, he lowered his head and gently touched her lips. She stood there suspended, while he moved his lips over hers. It was the sweetest kiss she had ever experienced. Then, it was over.

Her eyes fluttered open, only to find her hands on his shoulders in a death grip. She peered up at him, and found herself staring into an expression that could only be described as confused passion. He was the one breathing quickly now.

"Jeremy," she said breathlessly. She intended to say more, but thoughts had somehow escaped her.

At the sound of his name he seemed to come back to reality, and gently set her away from him, keeping one hand on her arm. He stared at her for a moment, then quietly asked, "Are you okay B?"

Maybe it was the endearing way he spoke to her, or the use of her nickname, but suddenly she was okay again. She took a deep breath of sea air, using it to strengthen her resolve.

"Yeah, I'm okay. I promise."

Whatever he saw on her face must have reassured him, because he let go of her arm. Then he grabbed her board and started walking back to the car.

"No! I need to surf!" she exclaimed, chasing after him.

"You're not surfing today Beth, no way!" he sternly told her.

He'd never spoken to her in absolutes, and she wanted to ask him who the hell he thought he was. But then a wave of exhaustion hit her, and she decided she was too tired to argue with him...today.

Later that night, while pushing her cooked carrots around on her plate, she thought again of the kiss she had shared with Jeremy.

"Hello, earth to Beth?" Mary said loudly.

"What? Oh, sorry Mom, I was just thinking," she said, a half smile still on her face.

"I can see that, and happy thoughts too. Care to share?" she asked, a mischievous look in her eyes.

"No."

"Fine, fine..but at some point you'll have to tell me who he is," her mother said, laughing at Beth's expression of surprise, "I'll always know you baby girl, it's just part of being a mother. Although, I have to admit, I can't seem to come up with a reason as to why you haven't eaten much of your dinner tonight."

Beth looked down at her plate, which was full of food. She had managed to eat a few carrots, a couple bites of pork chop and a scoop of applesauce. She glanced at her brother's plate, which was basically licked clean. "I'm just not feeling that well mom," she lied.

Mary looked at her, her eyebrows drawn together. "You seemed to look fine a few minutes ago when you were off in la la land."

"I know, but my stomach does hurt. I feel kind of nauseous actually." She watched as her mother's mild suspicion turned to genuine concern, and the guilt came rushing back.

"Here, I'll take your plate. You go upstairs and lie down. You've been studying and surfing so much, it's no wonder you're feeling a bit off."

"Thanks Mom," she said, ascending the stairs to her room.

She closed the door and leaned against it, feeling like shit, both physically and mentally. Her emotions had been reeling off course today, between what happened with Jeremy and lying to her mom. That combined with the crazy headache she had again from not eating was enough to make her want to just collapse in bed.

Unfortunately, research took precedence over bed tonight. She reviewed various websites about body mass index and ideal body weight for women. There were a lot of sites, but none of them specific for girls her age. She wrote down numbers from the sites about women and the sites about athletes. She even wrote down numbers from the sites about men. She stared at the numbers, her mind spinning. Finally, she worked out a chart that seemed reasonable for them to use. Then she fell into bed, weak and exhausted.

Four

The next morning, Beth hit her alarm and jumped out of bed, eager to get on the scale. Halfway across the room she was hit by a wave of dizziness. Holding onto the side of her dresser, she stood motionless until it passed. After a minute she felt more grounded, and headed to the bathroom. She was filled with elation to see she had lost two pounds! At this rate, she would definitely be ten pounds lighter by the end of the month. Quickly getting ready, she ate her grapefruit and headed out the door, water in hand. She picked up Jenny, counting the minutes until she could drop off Billy and start talking weight.

"I lost two pounds!" she exclaimed excitedly.

"I only lost one pound," Jenny said dejectedly. "My mom made lasagna, and I couldn't resist, I was so hungry. You know how good my mom's lasagna is!"

It was true, Jenny's mom's lasagna was literally award winning. Her mother was one hundred percent Italian, and two years ago she entered her lasagna into the local cooking contest. Her recipe had been passed down from generation to generation. It had won first place.

"Your mom kind of put you in a no-win situation," Beth said with a laugh. "No worries, up until that point, you hadn't eaten very much." She thought for a moment. "You only had one piece, right?"

Jenny gave her a guilty look, and Beth burst out laughing. "Okay, okay...well, at least you went running yesterday. You're challenge is going to be figuring out a way to escape your mother's cooking!"

"That's what scares me," Jenny mumbled. "Look at my dad!"

Beth smiled, thinking about Mr. Sullivan. The poor man had started out as a trim and attractive young man who had fallen in love with a beautiful Italian girl. Although still attractive for his age, his waistline was evidence that he had thoroughly enjoyed his wife's talent in the kitchen. Jenny had not only inherited his dark blond hair and green eyes, but also his love for her mother's cooking. As much as Jenny was her father physically, inside she was her mother...all high energy and at times, loud.

"I wonder how Mel and Rach did?" Beth muttered.

The answer to that came as soon as they pulled into the parking lot. Melanie ran up excitedly saying, "Rachel lost three pounds! Three pounds in a day! Can you believe it?"

Beth couldn't believe it. "What did you eat yesterday Rach?" she asked.

"The granola bar at lunch, water and an apple," she said, looking triumphant. Beth must have looked alarmed, because Rachel quickly said, "Hey, I feel fine. It's cool, no worries."

Beth turned to Melanie and asked, "How about you?"

Melanie looked around and quietly said, "I couldn't do it. I was so hungry. I think I actually gained a pound."

Beth put her arm around her and said, "Hey, it's totally fine. This is something I want to do, you do not have to do it with me. You are so beautiful Mel, you don't even need to lose one pound."

Melanie smiled, accepting herself.

Rachel stared at Melanie, loving and hating her at the same time.

Melanie had always been the confident one, almost fearless at times. Through the years, her sense of self had grown right along with her legs. With each new experience that was presented, she was always the first to jump in. As much as she loved her friends, she didn't need them in order to function. She was quite happy on her own, trying new things, meeting new people, always eager to learn. Her parents were still married, and from everything Rachel had seen over the years, they seemed happy. They were incredibly supportive of Melanie, never missing a soccer game, school play or anything that involved Melanie or her little sister.

And, yes, there were times Rachel hated her for it. She hated the close relationship Melanie had with her father, she hated her sweet and generous nature, but mostly, she hated how much she loved Melanie. Over the years, she had always stood up for Rachel. Her house was like a second home, and her parents had always been open and loving to her. Rachel knew she could count on Melanie for anything, just as Rachel would do anything for her.

"That's right Mel," she said, wrapping her arm around Melanie's waist, "you're perfect exactly as you are."

Melanie smiled at Rachel and gave her a small hug in return.

"Come on guys," Jenny yelled as she ran towards the school. The other three followed.

"Where's Beth?" Jeremy asked the girls for the second time.

"I don't know Jeremy, Jeez! What's up with you anyway?" Rachel asked, eyeing him suspiciously.

Jeremy's green eyes darted away from Rachel's blue ones. "Nothing, I just have to ask her something." He looked back at the girls, who all had knowing looks, especially Jenny. Raking his hand through his hair, he said, "Listen, I'm going to get in line, where are you guys eating?"

Suddenly they seemed very uncomfortable, and began glancing at each other. He watched the exchange with a mixture of annoyance and bafflement. He sighed.

"Look, tell Beth I'm looking for her, okay?"

The girls nodded in unison.

"Okay, that was weird," Jenny said, watching Jeremy stalk off. "We need to be more prepared in the future."

"Ya think?" Rachel said sarcastically, "The more weight we drop, the more questions people will have."

"Hey!" Beth hollered from the door. The girls watched as she worked her way through the lunch room. "What's up?" she asked when she finally reached them.

"Jeremy's looking for your ass...and when I say your ass, I mean he's literally looking for your ass!" Rachel said, glancing meaningfully at Beth's butt.

Melanie smiled, and asked, "What is going on with you two?"

Beth, who had given Rachel a shove, bit her lip and said, "I don't know." The other girls smiled again. Eager to change the subject, she said, "What have we agreed on for lunch?"

"Well, they have apples...we could eat some fruit," Jenny suggested.

Melanie scanned the selections. "You guys, I'm so hungry! I'm gonna get a sandwich, okay?"

The girls stared at her, and Melanie looked down, feeling guilty.

"Hey, go get your sandwich while we figure this out. Meet us outside," Rachel told her.

Melanie smiled and went to get in line.

"I don't know how I'm going to be able to eat with her!" Jenny said a little frantically. "A sandwich sounds so good!"

"We'll be fine," Beth said, "let's go to the salad bar and see what we can create."

They each made a salad of veggies, with no dressing. As she was getting her money out to pay, she heard a soft, deep voice behind her say, "I've been looking for you." She already knew who it was, and glanced over her shoulder with a smile.

"And you've found me," she said, pushing her tray forward towards the waiting cashier.

"Are you surfing today?" he asked.

She didn't answer immediately, focusing her attention on paying for lunch. She wanted to burn off calories, and surfing was always her first choice of exercise. But she couldn't risk being alone with Jeremy again, not yet. She needed to wrap her head around what was happening between them. It was very bad timing, she thought to herself as she began walking through the lunchroom towards the door leading outside. She had just embarked on a new journey of weight loss, which required a complete commitment from her. She wasn't sure she could handle two new experiences simultaneously...at least not if she wanted any success.

"Well??" Jeremy asked again, balancing his own tray and keeping up with her as she scooted through the maze of students.

"No, I'm going running with Jenny today," she said matter-of-factly, hoping he would let matters drop, yet knowing he wouldn't.

"Hey, wait a minute, will ya?" he said loudly as her paced increased. "Beth!" he snapped.

There it was again, that tone. That commanding tone.

Stopping, she turned and pinned him with her brown eyes. He stiffened. She hadn't looked at him like that since he broke the head off her favorite Barbie when they were eight. At least she stopped, he decided, walking over to her.

"Yeah? What is so important that you need to yell at me like that in front of everyone?" she said calmly...too calmly.

He glanced around, and saw a couple kids staring at them. "I'm sorry, B...I just want a few minutes alone with you. To talk," he clarified when he saw her expression change from annoyance to apprehension, of him. He didn't understand her lately, which was throwing him completely off balance. He knew she was keeping something from him. He assumed her friends knew, were even in on it, whatever "it" was. "I just want to talk, okay?" he asked again, smiling reassuringly.

Ever since they were five, his smile had always won her over. It still did. Only now, she noticed he had really beautiful lips, full yet masculine. She shook herself, realizing she was not only smiling back at him, but staring at his mouth like an idiot. She straightened, composing herself, and looked back at him with raised eyebrows.

"I have fifteen minutes before Jenny and I go running. Meet me outside the girls locker room," she ordered, deciding that if he wanted to boss her around, she could throw a little of it his way. She turned to leave, hoping that her order had pricked him a bit, but couldn't resist stealing a quick glance back to catch his reaction. She was a little disappointed to see a relieved smile on his face, not a frustrated brow as she was hoping.

"Where the hell were you?" Rachel asked as Beth sat down.

A courtyard that held outside tables was situated in the middle of their school. Being that it was September, one of the hottest months in Florida, most kids chose the comfort of air conditioning to eat lunch. As a result, they were alone.

"Nowhere, I was getting my lunch!" Beth snapped back. "Jeez Rach, testy much?"

"I'm sorry, it's just that you were going to tell us what you found out last night," Rachel said, sighing. "I have a headache."

"Have you taken anything for it?" Melanie asked, concerned. "I have some Advil in my locker."

"No, but I'm fine. Let's get down to business."

Beth finished chewing a mouthful of salad, and began to tell them everything she had read. "So, your stats are your height and weight, obviously. The amount of weight each of us should lose will be different, because we are different heights. Well, except Melanie and me, but she's not doing it."

Melanie nodded, her mouth full of sandwich.

Rachel stared at her, chewing on a piece of carrot. She dragged her gaze away from Melanie's sandwich and asked Beth, "So, what's yours?"

"Well, I'm five feet-four inches, so my ideal weight is anywhere between, like, 110 – 145 pounds. I'm at 118 now, which is after the two pounds I've already lost. I can't imagine being 145, can you?" she asked the girls. They emphatically shook their heads. "So my goal weight is 110 pounds," she said, smiling and shoving another piece of salad in her mouth.

"That would put you at the very bottom of your range," Melanie mumbled, stating the obvious.

Beth nodded, still chewing. "Exactly!" she said around a mouthful of food, "I would be the thinnest I could be, safely."

Melanie thought on that. "Well, as long as you stay in your range. You don't want to end up like one of those super skinny girls, they look so unhealthy!"

Beth rolled her eyes and took another bite.

"Where am I supposed to be at?" Rachel asked.

"Hold on, I wrote you guys down," she said, pulling a piece of paper out of her pocket. "Okay, Rachel...you are five feet-six inches so your range is between, like 118 – 153 pounds."

"Really?" Rachel asked, looking thoughtful. "Hm, I'm 121 now, and that's after losing three pounds. I could easily get to 118, no prob!"

She smiled then, a real, true smile. The other girls smiled back. Rachel wasn't the most jovial one of the group, mainly due to her home life. Her friends had always accepted that. No conditions had ever been placed on her to be happier or more upbeat. Still, when they did see her genuinely pleased about something, it made them happy.

"But, just like Beth, you can't go below your range Rach, promise?" Melanie asked, her dark eyes looking very pointedly at Rachel.

"I know, I know Mel, relax already!" she said, waving her off. "Okay, what about Jenny?"

Jenny turned to Beth, excitedly waiting for her stats. "Jenny, you are five feet-two inches so your range is between, like 104 – 135 pounds."

Jenny's shoulders slumped, "I'm 130 pounds as it is! I didn't realize I had gotten so fat!"

"You are not fat Jenny!" Melanie said.

"Yes I am, and you guys know it! I've always been the fattest one out of the four of us!" she said loudly. She sat up straight and said, "That's it, no more cheating! I'm going to get thin!"

"That's good Jen, but remember-" Melanie began.

"I know, I know Mel! I'm not the one you have to worry about, I have plenty of fat on me to spare!" she shouted, then quickly covered her mouth, looking around. Seeing the courtyard empty, she smiled with relief.

Beth finished her third water bottle of the day walking out of English, her last class. She opened her locker, shoved in her books and grabbed her gym bag. Taking a deep breath, she headed toward the girls locker room and contemplated the impending conversation with Jeremy. It could go two ways, either he wanted to know what she was hiding from him, or he wanted to talk about their kiss on the beach. She had every intention of avoiding both topics.

Turning the corner, she saw him leaning against the wall outside the locker room, waiting for her. His head was bent in thought, and his dark hair hung across his brow. One foot rested on the wall and his hands were shoved in his pockets. He glanced in her direction, and immediately straightened, pushing himself away from the wall. His gaze roamed over her appreciatively as she walked toward him. She wished he wouldn't look at her like that, because it seemed to cause her to blush.

"Hey," she said, looking up at him, smiling.

"Hey," he said, smiling back.

God, she was beautiful! How he missed it all these years, he'd never know. Even though her big brown eyes were obviously her most prominent feature, the rest of her face was just as gorgeous. She had smooth skin, arched brows, a small, yet full mouth and a pretty nose. Her hair fell around her face and down her back in thick chestnut waves. That combined with one hell of a body didn't help his peace of mind. He struggled to regain focus while she looked up at him expectantly.

"Yeah, so how's it goin'?" he began, feeling truly awkward around her for the first time in his life.

She gave a light laugh, "Good...how's it goin' for you?" she asked, raising her eyebrows, smiling.

"Good, good..good," he started rambling, then quickly shut his mouth. It was time to grow some balls and just get on with it! He took a deep breath, looked back down at her and blurted, "Are you doing anything tomorrow night?"

He was asking her out, like on a real date! At least that's what it sounded like. She thought she better make sure, so she asked, "Um, no. Why?"

The relief he had felt after finally getting up the nerve to ask her swiftly left him. She needed clarification? He assumed his intentions were fairly clear at this point.

"Well, I thought maybe we could go to Opus...you know, for dinner," he added, just in case she wasn't sure why they would be going to a restaurant.

Beth was stunned, and a strange kind of what could only be described as...happy.

She gave him a smile that was so big, so shining that Jeremy felt himself almost sway. He watched her lips say, "Sure, what time?"

"How about seven?" he asked.

"Sounds great!" she said, and quickly looked around. Seeing the hallway deserted, she leaned up on her tiptoes. Thinking she was going to whisper something in his ear, he leaned down. The secret he expected was forgotten as he felt her soft lips on his. It only lasted a second, and then she was gone.

Jeremy straightened, and was sure he was standing taller than before.

"So...I was thinking...I don't know how I'm going to keep avoiding...you know...eating dinner," Beth said to Jenny, in between breaths. They had been running around the track for thirty minutes.

"I know what you mean...I don't know..what to do either," Jenny said. "Obviously..the longer..we do this..the harder it's gonna be..to hide."

"Yeah," Beth panted.

It was actually going to be a big problem for both of them. Unlike Rachel, Beth and Jenny sat down to dinner most nights with their families.

"If I even hint...to my mom that I'm on a diet...she will totally watch my weight."

"Well....I could tell my parents... I just want to lose a couple pounds.... so I'm watching what I'm eating.... more closely. Even they would have to agree... I could spare a few," Jenny said matter of factly.

Beth was envious, because she couldn't use that excuse. Her mother would never agree that she needed to lose weight. She was just going to have to continue to play the "sick" card she threw out last night and see how long it lasted. If she went surfing, especially with Jeremy, she could say she ate beforehand. Her mom didn't like her ruining her appetite for dinner, so she would have to be very strategic with that excuse. She was sure avoiding her mother's watchful eye was going to be a constant issue.

"Oh..Jeremy and I are going on a date...tomorrow night!" she yelled over her shoulder, increasing her speed for their final lap.

Jenny, who had hesitated after hearing that amazing revelation, sped back up. Beth had finished the last lap, and was walking around in a circle to cool down. She smiled as Jenny approached at a sprint, skidding to a stop in front of her.

"What?" Jenny panted loudly. After a few more breaths, she said again, "What??"

Beth began stretching, "I said, Jeremy and I are going on a date tomorrow night. He asked me out!"

Jenny observed her friend's smile, noting that her eyes shined right along with it. She laughed to herself as she began warming down. It made sense, they were perfect for each other. No matter how many rifts the four of them got in over the years, Jeremy always remained true to Beth. There were many times Jenny had been frustrated with his blind loyalty to Beth, always coming to her defense, even when she was at fault. He had probably been in love with her even then.

"I'm really happy for you B," Jenny said quietly, smiling.

Beth stopped in mid-stretch, and looked at her.

"It's only a date Jen, he didn't propose!"

Jenny's smile widened, because she was sure a proposal from Jeremy was in Beth's future.

"Come on, I'll buy you an apple and water to celebrate!" she said, laughing.

"Can you throw in some Advil too?" Beth asked, pinching the bridge of her nose. "These headaches keep coming back. It's from restricting calories. Are you getting them?"

Jenny shook her head, "Not yet, and I hope I don't. I have been dizzy off and on. I just drink more water."

"Well, we should drink a lot of water after exercising. I'll take you up on your offer," Beth told her as they headed to the snack bar. "We need to stop by Rachel's on the way home, she forgot her English book."

The sounds of Joan Osbourne filled Rachel's head. As usual, she had escaped to her room almost immediately after getting home from school. With an apple and water in hand, she had locked the door, laid on her bed and turned up her iPod.

Her mother's latest boyfriend was a firefighter, which allowed him to be off for a couple days at a time. Rachel didn't know where he lived, but apparently, he now lived with them, at least for the time being. She really hated this one, mainly due to his penchant for leering. It actually made her want to puke.

"Rachel...Rachel!" someone was yelling at her. Rachel's eyes snapped open, and she pulled her iPod out of her ears.

She opened her door to find Beth and Jenny standing there, laughing. "Jeez," Beth said, "How loud do you have that thing?"

"Trust me, not loud enough," Rachel muttered. Then she said, very loudly, "Did you meet the latest jerk?"

Jenny shut the door, an alarmed look on her face. "Rachel, you don't want him to hear you!"

"Why not? What do I care? He'll be gone soon enough. I think he's on week three...I give him two more weeks, then she'll move on to another one," she said matter of factly, sitting back down on her bed.

Beth smiled grimly. She knew Rachel would reject pity, so she was always careful to hide it, even though she felt it. From the time Rachel was two, her home environment had been chaos. Her dad had left one day, and just never came back. Simple as that. A letter had arrived within a week informing his wife that he had begun divorce proceedings.

Her mother, terrified her social status would diminish once people learned of the abandonment of her husband, immediately set out to find another one. Her efforts failed, so she turned her obsession from finding a husband to holding onto her youth. Over the years, the girls had witnessed the transformation of Mrs. Emerson's face as a result of too much plastic surgery. Living off the alimony and child support she received as part of the divorce settlement, her mother spent her days either at the spa, club or gym.

Rachel had mostly raised herself, with the occasional nanny thrown in for good measure. She had only spoken of her father once, when they were ten. Beth had been showing them pictures from her grandparents trip to Australia, and Rachel had quietly said, "I think my dad lives there, or in Europe."

The three of them went silent, staring at Rachel, waiting for her to say more. She didn't, and the matter was dropped, never to be brought up again.

"You know I hate it when you look at me like that B," Rachel said as she leaned over to set her iPod on the nightstand.

"What look?" Beth asked innocently, remembering for the hundredth time that she could never get anything past her.

Rachel gave her an you-know-what-I-mean-look. "Why'd you guys stop by?"

Beth threw the English book towards her. "You left it on your desk and we have a test tomorrow."

Rachel tossed the book near her iPod, "I've already read it, twice."

"Oh," Beth said.

Rachel's intellect never seemed to surprise her, but she hadn't considered Rachel would have read *The Bell Jar* for pleasure.

"Have you read it?" she asked.

Beth rolled her eyes and said, "Of course not, you know I haven't."

Instead of teasing her, as she expected, Rachel just nodded. "You should, it's actually very good."

They were interrupted by laughter and commotion coming from the living room.

"He and his buddy are just drinking, no big deal," she answered their unspoken question.

"Rachel," Jenny hesitantly began, "Do you ever feel...unsafe?"

Surprised, Beth looked at Jenny. As loud as Jenny could be sometimes, courage was not one of her strong suits. She looked at Rachel, curious to hear the answer.

"No..no, they're harmless. As long as I stay out of their way...out of my mother's way to be more specific, it's like I'm not here. Really, they all pretty much ignore me," she explained, as if it was all a normal part of family life.

Beth glanced at Jenny, who didn't seem to like Rachel's answer, which was reflected in her face. Not wanting Rachel to see it, Beth changed the subject, quickly.

"So, guess who I'm going out with tomorrow night?" she asked Rachel, who had been observing Jenny's reaction out of the corner of her eye.

She turned her full attention to Beth. "Who?" she asked, genuinely surprised.

"Jeremy!" Jenny shrieked before Beth could answer.

Rachel's mouth actually fell open, "No way!" she yelled, pushing Beth.

"Yep," Beth said, feeling a little cocky. Then her bravado fell and she started giggling. "Can you believe it?"

Rachel, who was now smiling, thought for a minute. "You know B, I can. I can believe it. Yeah," she said, warming up to the subject, "I'd say it's about damn time!"

"That's how I felt," Jenny said, smiling.

Beth looked at them, smiling back. Not due to her upcoming date with Jeremy, but because of the obvious love they felt for her, and she for them.

Rachel waved goodbye to her friends as they drove away and shut the front door. She turned to find her mom's boyfriend, and his friend, standing directly in front of her.

"Yes?" she asked in her most annoyed voice.

The friend looked her up and down, rubbing his chin. Bile rose up in her throat. "What do you want?" she said quickly, hoping she could keep the beginnings of fear at bay.

Her mom's boyfriend leaned closer and said, "We were just wondering if you want to take a dip in the pool with us?"

She turned her face away from the stench of beer. "No, thanks anyways," she said, trying to sound bored.

Her hands were still holding onto the doorknob behind her, and for a fleeting second she considered running out of the house, screaming for help. Worried that the fear and anxiety she was feeling would overtake her, she stood up straighter, drawing on strength she didn't know she possessed.

"Please get out of my way, I have homework to do. Now!" she added when they didn't move.

The friend moved back slightly, and bowed drunkenly as she passed. Her mom's boyfriend calmly watched her escape to her room, like she was a little bug that he could capture at his whim.

She slammed the door behind her, locked it and held her breath. Only after she heard them leave did she dare to open the door again. The house was empty. She ran to the front door and locked it, knowing it was a pointless gesture because the jerk already had a key to the house.

She went back to her room, quickly turning the lock behind her. She leaned her head against the door and braced herself. It started in the pit of her stomach, and spiraled out into her being. She doubled over with it, and began to sob. Then she began screaming.

The pain was too much, too real. She was sure the hopelessness she was feeling, the utter lack of control over her own life, was going to take her this time. She looked wildly about her room, not knowing what she was searching for, yet knowing.

Her search led her to the bathroom connected to her room.

With tears streaming down her face, she opened the top drawer and reached in. Finding what she was looking for, she leaned against the wall opposite the mirror...getting control of her tears, putting the pain back inside, hiding it again.

She reminded herself that she couldn't let it escape like this. If her mother ever decided to pay her some attention, and witnessed an outburst like the one she just had, she'd have her committed. The fact that Rachel demanded almost nothing allowed her mother to tolerate her. If she were to embarrass her mother in front of the many men who traipsed through their home, she would be gone.

She slid down the wall, and pushed strands of black hair out of her eyes. Sitting on the floor, she rolled her sleeve until it was almost over her shoulder. She chose a razor blade out of the baggy, and pressed it into her upper arm. She pressed and pressed, matching the physical pain to the pain she was feeling inside her soul. The relief was immediate, like a balloon releasing some of its air. Not enough though. She cut another line below the first one, and leaned her head back, letting the calmness take effect. She glanced down, noticing the drops of blood on her arm. This was a bad one. Sometimes she bled, sometimes she was just left with a deep mark in her skin. Grabbing a towel off the bar above her head, she pressed it against her arm, wiping away the blood. Her breathing slowed, the tears dried, and Rachel let the numbness wash over her.

***

"See ya!" Beth yelled out her car window after she dropped off Jenny.

Instantly her mind jumped ahead to the upcoming meal she was expected to share with her mom and brother. She had done really good today, fruit for breakfast, salad for lunch and fruit for snack. That, combined with the run, should almost guarantee some serious weight loss! She just had to get through dinner.

The smell of it hit her in the face as soon as she entered the house, and Beth began to fear something more than her mother's attentiveness. She feared herself. Because at that moment, she felt like she could eat twenty cheeseburgers! Her body's response to the smell of food was instant, and she wasn't so sure she could play the sick card tonight.

"Hey Mom, what's for dinner?" she asked, already knowing it was her mother's famous turkey burgers. Damn, Beth thought to herself, eyeing the homemade French fries on the counter.

"Your favorite, turkey burgers!" her mother exclaimed with a smile. "And French fries!"

"I see that," Beth said, returning her mom's smile, although, not quite as enthusiastically.

"I hope you're feeling better honey. I'd hate to see all this yummy food go to waste!"

Beth knew she was going to be good and well tonight. How bad could one turkey burger be, anyway?

Later, in her room, she wasn't so sure about her decision to eat a burger. Her stomach ached so bad, she thought it was going to burst. The handful of fries she'd eaten was only adding to her misery.

The guilt over eating wasn't helping matters either. It was a new emotion for her. Never in her life had she felt guilt when it came to food, or eating. The fact that she was feeling it now, and strongly, was a little disturbing. And although she wasn't enjoying the state she was in, she couldn't seem to shrug it off either. She assumed guilt and anxiety must go hand in hand when someone was on a diet. She had been experiencing a lot of the latter, and now the former had just introduced itself.

Compulsion was also in there somewhere, she realized, frantically trying to figure out a way not to gain any weight from the dinner she had enjoyed. She glanced at the clock, seven o' clock shined back at her. She could throw on her suit and swim laps for thirty minutes. Her mom couldn't object to her taking a quick dip. In fact, Beth decided as she started to get undressed, her mother would probably be happy she was actually using the pool!

"I feel like a swim!" she announced, breezing by her mom, who was sitting with Billy on the couch.

"At this hour?" Mary asked.

"Yeah, why not? It's still light out...sorta," she said over her shoulder as she headed out the slider.

Her mom and brother looked at each other.

"Do you want to go swimming?" Mary asked her son.

Billy shook his head so hard that she burst out laughing.

Beth pushed and pushed, swimming lap after lap, until she felt less full. Less fat. Forty-five minutes later, she slowly walked back up to her room, completely exhausted.

Five

The next morning, she went through her routine of running to the bathroom before anyone was up. She pulled the scale out as quietly as she could and got on. She'd lost another pound! She couldn't believe it. She was sure that the turkey burger and fries had thrown all her hard work off. Thank God she had decided to swim, it probably saved her.

She floated around the house, marveling at how giddy she felt, how accomplished she felt, just by losing another pound. It was like she was on some sort of high. She waited until her mom left for work, then ate her grapefruit. Billy just rolled his eyes at her and made a face at the grapefruit.

"Okay, how much?" Jenny asked after they dropped off Billy. It was becoming their normal morning conversation.

"One pound, and I'm actually excited about it. I ate dinner last night, like, really ate," Beth confessed.

Jenny raised her eyebrows in surprise. "I didn't, and I lost two pounds, finally!" she said excitedly.

Beth was happy for her. "How did you get out of dinner?"

"My parents had to go to some dinner party for my dad's work, so they weren't home! My mom told me to make mac and cheese, which I didn't of course. She didn't even question me about it because they got home so late. It was perfect!"

After a moment, she added, "I did feel kind of sick though, you know, like weak sick. And really dizzy. I didn't like that. I drank a diet soda, which helped, a little. I had a bad headache by the time I went to bed. I couldn't wait to eat my fruit this morning! At least I lost weight though, right?"

Beth nodded as she drove into a parking space at school. Rachel and Melanie were waiting for them.

"How much Rach?" Beth asked.

Rachel gave her a smug smile, "Two more pounds!"

Beth's mouth dropped open. "Two more pounds? How are you losing more than us, we are all eating the same, basically. Did you have dinner?"

"Sort of," Rachel said.

"What does that mean?" Melanie asked as they walked into school.

"It means I sort of ate, here and there. Don't worry Mel!" she said in response to Melanie's worried frown.

The bell rang, and the girls went to their classes.

"So what ya wearing tonight?" Melanie asked Beth, biting into a piece of pizza.

They were sitting at their now regular table outside, eating their salads. All except Melanie. Beth stared at the pizza, her mouth beginning to water.

"What?" she asked.

"What are you wearing tonight?" Melanie repeated.

Beth sat back, thoughtfully chewing a carrot. "I don't know. He's seen me in almost everything."

"You should wear something hot, you know, something low cut...and tight jeans!" Jenny said, smiling.

Rachel rolled her eyes.

Beth laughed. She did have one shirt that she knew for sure Jeremy had never seen. Her parents had bought it for her when they had all gone to her cousin's wedding in Vegas. The only reason her mom had let her keep it was because Beth had promised not to wear it again until she was eighteen.

"You're right Jen, thanks."

"You're very welcome!" Jenny said, digging into her salad. "Are we running today?"

Beth was dying to surf, but didn't want to see Jeremy before their date.

"Yeah, let's run. You guys wanna run with us?" she asked Rachel and Melanie.

"I'll go!" Melanie said. "I have my stuff here already for gym, so I'll just use that."

Beth turned to Rachel.

"No, thanks. You know I'm not the running type. Anyway, I have plans," she muttered.

She said the last so quietly, Beth almost missed it. All three of them leaned in and said, "What?"

Rachel looked back at them. "I have plans, don't look so surprised! It happens, sometimes."

Her friends looked at each other, then at her, expectantly.

She looked up at the sky and gave a loud sigh. "Corey LaSalle," she said, and started laughing at the looks on their faces. She had always been good at surprising them.

Beth was the first to speak. "Corey? But he's a surfer, and you hate the beach."

Rachel smiled. It was true, she did hate the beach. But she loved Corey's hazel eyes, and he was always so nice to her. He was almost...gentle towards her. Most boys that were interested in her were quickly scared away by her confident demeanor and edgy exterior. She wasn't attracted to the boys that were similar to her in temperament. As a result, Rachel didn't have many dates.

No one was more surprised than Rachel when Corey began talking to her, hesitantly at first, but then on a more regular basis. When he looked at her, it was almost like he saw past all of her....damage. To him, it seemed, she was just a girl. A simple girl, no past, no issues.

Rachel didn't realize how badly she needed someone to see her like that until the day he asked her out. She said yes before he finished the sentence. She didn't mean to. She bit her lip as soon as the word was out of her mouth, fully expecting him to see her as desperate. He had just smiled warmly, and kissed her on the cheek.

"What can I say? My tastes have changed."

Beth stared at her. Rachel had a fear of the ocean since they were little. Whenever the four of them went to the beach, they had to sit as far away as humanly possible from the water. Rachel would sit in her beach chair, contentedly reading a book, watching her friends swim and surf. In fact, whenever they were at the beach, they nicknamed Rachel "Mom" because she looked just like all the other mothers sitting on the beach, watching their children play.

Beth also knew Corey, not as well as she knew Rachel of course, but well enough. She had surfed with him many times, and she liked him, a lot. He was a good guy. He was also a friend of Jeremy's, and she trusted Jeremy's judgment in most things. She just never would have put Rachel and Corey together, ever.

"Are you done analyzing the situation?" Rachel asked Beth with a smile.

Beth laughed, "Yeah."

"And what conclusions did you come to, may I ask?" she asked, watching Beth closely.

"I think Corey is a great guy," Beth began, the other two girls nodding, "and I think we should double date sometime!"

Rachel's smile widened, and she happily dug into her salad.

Beth dusted her cheeks with a little blush, and leaned back to observe her appearance. She had taken extra care with her hair, using loads of conditioner to make it soft, and brushing it over and over until it shined. She thought about putting it up, but had a memory of a time she had caught Jeremy staring at her hair when he thought she wasn't looking. Apparently, he liked her hair, so she was leaving it down for him.

Normally she didn't wear much make-up, if any at all, so her eyes were looking especially big with the little bit of shadow and mascara she had used. The blush added a glow to her already lightly tanned face. All that was missing was lip gloss, which she usually wore. Even though her lips were full, her mouth was kind of small, forcing her to always wear either lip gloss or lipstick in order for her mouth not to get lost.

She dabbed a little blush between her breasts, which were pushed up nicely by her bra. Other than a bikini, Jeremy had never seen her wear anything so revealing. The shirt was a basic black, but the material had a shimmer that created a very feminine effect when the light hit it. The sleeves lay delicately on her arms, almost touching her elbows. Besides the deep vee in the front, the rest of the shirt was very simple, except for the fact that it fit her body like a glove. She had chosen her best pair of jeans, the ones that made her butt look absolutely fantastic. A pair of sexy black sling backs finished the ensemble. Yes, she thought to herself, this outfit would do quite well!

The doorbell rang, and she stifled the urge to run out of her room and down the stairs to see his reaction. Calmly she grabbed her denim clutch, opened the door, and began to leave. As an after-thought, she ran back into her room and sprayed a little perfume on her wrists, and between her breasts. Satisfied, she gave her hair a shake and proceeded down the stairs.

She heard voices coming from the living room and could already picture Jeremy lounging on the couch, talking to her mom and brother. Her house had always been his second home, so she knew he wasn't one bit nervous waiting for her to come down.

On that count, Beth could not have been more wrong. Jeremy's stomach was in knots, and he was having a hard time concentrating on what Mrs. Baxter was saying. It didn't help that Billy had asked Jeremy to play a video game with him. Between trying to answer Mrs. Baxter's questions, and hit a tennis ball with his remote, his head was spinning! And that was before Beth walked in, looking more like a woman than a sixteen-year-old girl.

He just stood there, taking her in, while Billy yelled at him that he missed the shot. His head began to feel a little funny, and he realized he had stopped breathing. Thankfully, Mrs. Baxter spoke first, because he was still trying to catch his breath.

"Beth, I thought we had an agreement on that shirt," Mary said quietly as she approached her daughter.

Beth looked at her mom beseechingly. "Please Mom, please?" she pleaded. When her mother continued to stare at her, she said, "Come on Mom, it's Jeremy. If you can't trust me with him, who can you trust me with?"

Her mother thought on that for a moment, then must have come to the same conclusion. She nodded, kissed Beth on the forehead and told them both to have a good time.

Jeremy opened the car door for her, and Beth felt like a princess. She felt dizzy too, but chose to ignore that.

"Beth, you look...you look amazing," he said quietly after they had driven for a few minutes.

She glanced at him. He wore a soft green shirt that matched his eyes. It hugged his muscular shoulders and chest, fitting him loosely down to his hips. His faded jeans fit him perfectly, and she suppressed a smile as she saw even going out to dinner, Jeremy wore flip flops. They were nice flip flops though.

"You look very nice too Jeremy," she said shyly, and she meant it. He did look nice, damn nice.

He looked at her, offering her a crooked smile, and a lock of his dark hair fell across his forehead. "Not as good as you though, trust me. You're going to set the place on fire."

It was quiet for a moment, then they both started laughing.

"You know, I've never said anything like that before," he said, still laughing.

"I've never actually heard anyone say it, at least not in real life!" she said through her giggles.

They both relaxed, the tension having been broken.

Opus was Beth's favorite restaurant. They had gone there with their families when they were little, but had never gone alone, just the two of them. Jeremy was happy...no, proud, to walk in with her.

"What are you going to have?" he asked after they were seated.

Beth stared at the menu. Her excitement over the date had eclipsed everything else in her mind, including the fact that she was going to have to figure out how to eat, or rather, not eat, with him. There was no way she could eat a full meal, not after the burger and fries she'd had the night before. For one, she wanted to make sure she was going to weigh less when she stepped on the scale in the morning, and secondly, there wasn't a pool outside the restaurant to swim laps.

"Ummmm, I don't know," she said slowly. "I'm not starving...maybe I'll just order a salad," she finished brightly, looking across the table at him.

He was looking at her like she was crazy, and told her so.

"Are you nuts? I'm sorry Beth, but there's no way you're only having a salad. Come on," he continued, "you know how good the food is here."

She did know, the food was wonderful. Dammit, but she hated this. "Do you want to share something? I'm really not that hungry."

Jeremy stared across the table at her. The waiter came to take their drink order, and he ordered sparkling water, sodas and an order of fried calamari for an appetizer. After the waiter left, he looked back at her, challenging.

"We are going to have a nice dinner together B, we are going to eat, drink and be merry. I don't want to hear how you aren't hungry, or you already ate, or whatever. Got it?"

Beth wished the waiter would hurry up and bring her drink, so she could throw it at him. She decided that as soon as they had a private moment, she was going to explain to him, very firmly, that she didn't like being ordered about. But at the moment, he had her trapped, and his demands were almost more than she could bear.

She looked down, knowing she wasn't going to win this one. Her eyes scanned the menu, looking at her favorite dishes. Grilled Salmon, Linguini with Pesto, Chicken Marsala.....Chicken Marsala. Her father's favorite. Images of her father enjoying his Chicken Marsala during one of their numerous visits to Opus flashed across her mind.

Blinking quickly so as not to shed the tears that had begun to fill her eyes, she looked up at him and quietly said, "It's just that..I'm trying to..you know...lose a little weight."

Jeremy, who had been teasing, realized he had somehow upset her. He leaned forward and took her hand, "Beth, I didn't mean to upset you. I'm sorry," he said tenderly, and the tears she had been fighting so hard to control began spilling down her cheeks. Quickly, she dabbed her eyes.

"No Jeremy, I'm sorry, I'm so sorry. Would you please excuse me a moment?" she asked.

"Of course," he said, standing up as she left. He studied her figure as she made her way to the ladies room. Beth had never been overweight, her body had always been well toned from running and surfing. He thought back, trying to conjure up memories of her dieting, and couldn't come up with a single one. This was definitely a new side to her.

She entered the ladies room, still trying to get a hold on her emotions. She was more frustrated with herself than with Jeremy. Closing her eyes, she took a deep breath…Jeremy. How sweet he had been, and how gentle, when he realized she was crying.

She looked at herself in the mirror. Some of her mascara had begun to streak under her eyes. "What are you doing?" she asked, searching her reflection for a hint of an answer.

She was ruining a beautiful night, one he had planned just for her. Why couldn't she just let her diet go for tonight? And why did it not quite feel like a diet anymore, but more of an obsession? It was true, she had never officially been on a diet, but her mom had done Weight Watchers, and her aunt was always on some sort of diet. They would be the first ones to put their diets on hold if there was a special occasion, or if they went out to dinner. The diet didn't control them.

She was definitely starting to feel controlled. Instantly, she straightened. If there was one thing Beth loved, it was her independence and the light feeling she usually carried with her that resulted from knowing who she was and what she wanted out of life. She didn't like the fact that food was somehow starting to hinder that part of her spirit.

Yet, if she was truly honest with herself, her spirit had plummeted the day her father left. She stood there, staring at herself in the ladies room.

For the first time in her life, Beth wasn't one hundred percent sure who she was or what she wanted. Except Jeremy, she definitely wanted Jeremy.

She wet a paper towel and fixed her make-up, shook out her hair and smiled. Tonight, she wouldn't think of anything except him. She would look into his eyes and gain the strength she needed to get through this dinner.

She walked back to the table, noticing that he was staring broodingly off into space.

"Hey, you awake?" she asked with a smile, sitting down. He sat up in his chair, smiling tentatively.

"Are you okay?" he asked, searching her face.

"I'm fine, no, I'm great...really." She reached across the table, took his hand and leaned as far forward as she could. Seeing her intention, he met her halfway.

The kiss she gave him was sweet and soft, and yet Jeremy felt like he was on fire. He was breathing a little faster as he leaned back into his chair, and was amazed he could react so strongly to her, especially in the middle of a restaurant. He was thankful for the distraction of the waiter approaching with their appetizer.

"This looks great!" she said excitedly, almost falling into the food as she dished some onto her plate.

He just shook his head in bemusement, and filled his own plate.

"Are you ready to order?" the waiter asked.

"Do you need more time?" Jeremy asked hesitantly, fearing she might dissolve into tears again at the mention of more food.

But she just shook her head, "No, I'm good," she said looking at the menu again. She sighed, "I'll have the salmon, the one with the asparagus, capers and lemon." Then she nodded her head, more to herself, and closed the menu so loudly that a couple from a nearby table looked at her. "Sorry," she said, biting her lip.

Jeremy gave his order of a steak, medium rare, baked potato, creamed spinach and a Caesar salad.

By the time he was done Beth's eyes were huge. "You're going to eat all that?" she asked disbelievingly.

Jeremy looked offended. "You don't think I can?" he asked as he handed the waiter his menu. "How do you think I grew so much over the summer? Remember, I'm a growing boy!"

They both laughed, and began eating their calamari. She cut hers into tiny bites, and took forever to chew each one. She listened as he regaled her with stories about the antics of his baseball teammates, loving the way his deep voice told the story. By the time their food arrived, she had managed to eat only two little calamaris. Not bad, she thought to herself as an idea formed. She did the same with her dinner, cutting up the asparagus into tiny bites, and picking off small bits of salmon.

Finding a groove with her dinner allowed her to converse with him. Before the date, she had wondered if talking to him now would be different than before...before they had kissed. She was not only relieved, but thrilled to realize they still clicked just as good as always.

Actually better, she thought for the tenth time that night, finding herself lost in his expressive eyes. He had her locked into his gaze, and for a brief moment she wondered if that was the expression he wore when having sex. Beth looked away, drawing her eyebrows together. Having sex? Where the heck did that thought come from?

She had never thought of sex. She had discussed it, many times, with her friends, but had never really imagined doing it. Until now. She took a sip of her diet soda while examining this new emotion. Until Jeremy. With an assurance she didn't know she possessed, she looked at him and knew, without a doubt, he was the one.

Jeremy, who was starting to ask her if she was going to Corey's party the next night, stopped in mid-sentence, and swallowed. He didn't think it was possible for Beth to look any more beautiful, but somehow, she did. The way she was looking at him made his mouth go dry.

"You were saying something?" she asked with an innocent smile.

He took a sip of his soda and cleared his throat. He sat there blankly, trying to remember what he had been about to ask her. "Oh yeah, are you going to Corey's party tomorrow night?"

"Yeah, we're going." Then her eyes brightened, as if remembering something important. "Did you know Rachel and Corey are dating?" she whispered across the table.

"No way, there's no way! She's not his type," Jeremy said with a dismissive shake of his head.

Beth raised one eyebrow and said, "Oh really? Then why are they out on a date tonight? And what do you mean "not his type?" You mean not some airhead, who isn't into surfing but is into surfers?"

He threw up his hands, laughing. "Relax, it's nothing against Rachel...really!" he said when she continued to stare at him. "It's just that, you know, she's not..." He thought for a moment, then looked at her in defeat, "An airhead who isn't into surfing, but is into surfers."

She burst out laughing.

"You wanna go to the beach?" he asked as they left the restaurant.

"Sure," Beth said, liking the idea. She had managed to only eat half her salmon and most of her asparagus. She felt full, but not super fat. A walk along the beach would help burn off some calories.

"Look at that moon! I think it's a harvest moon!" she exclaimed. Ever since she was a little girl, she had loved the moon, it was one of her favorite things.

"It's too early to be a harvest moon, that's not for another couple weeks," he corrected her.

She gave him a look that said *"I don't really care, it looks like a harvest moon to me."*

Jeremy was always informing her of the correct information, whether she asked for it or not. She never asked for it, but that never stopped him from sharing. She was sure there were times that he rambled off facts just to annoy her.

They sat down on the sand, staring at the moonlight reflecting off the water. The light from the pier, which was about a half mile away, shone on the ever present fisherman as they made their casts.

"Beth..." Jeremy began.

She looked at him, and the light breeze off the ocean blew strands of hair into her face. She moved her hand to get them, but he beat her to it. Gently, he put her hair back in place behind her ear.

"I should have brought a clip," she said breathlessly, still feeling the place where his hands had touched her hair.

He slowly shook his head. "No, I love it down, I've always loved your hair," he said quietly.

Beth didn't know what to say back to that. 'I've always loved your hair too' sounded kind of stupid. So she simply said, "Thank you."

He smiled, "Your welcome."

Then he wasn't smiling anymore, and his hand, which had somehow sunk into her hair, began to gently push her head toward his. Her eyes closed, and she lifted her mouth, knowing she was going to be kissed. She almost jumped when she felt his lips on her forehead, not her lips. Then she froze.

Jeremy gently kissed her forehead, her eyelids, her nose. Her breathing became shallow, and for a brief moment she felt like she was slowly swaying on a boat. Then he found her lips, and the swaying stopped. In its place was a feeling so electric that she was completely consumed by it. Their mouths intertwined, over and over again, and she found herself clasping him to her, losing her balance and pulling him down on top of her. Then everything changed.

He tore his mouth from hers and kissed her neck, over and over again. She dug her fingers into the hair at his nape. His hands moved down her body, past her hips, to her legs, then back up again. He kept kissing her and kissing her. He reached for her breast just as she arched her hips, and she heard him moan.

All of a sudden, he pushed himself up, and leaned back on his ankles. Staring down at her, he fought to get air into his lungs. *What had just happened?* he thought to himself. His desire for her had almost caused him to lose all reason. He loved her, and she deserved better, especially for her first time. He looked up at the black sky, and closed his eyes.

Through gossip, he had learned a lot about the girls at his school, and thankfully, Beth's name was rarely mentioned. When it was, it was usually to comment on her body, and one look from Jeremy always shut them up. What they had just done proved to him she was a virgin. Her reactions had been full of surprise and honesty. She hadn't known what was coming, or what to expect.

"What's wrong?" she asked breathlessly, sitting up.

Jeremy looked back at her, and smiled weakly. Even her voice turned him on. "Nothing,

nothing at all. We just need to slow down a little," he said, moving closer to her.

"Why?" she asked, her big brown eyes looking up at him.

Yeah, why Jeremy? he thought to himself, then shook his head as if to clear it. "Because, we may not stop," he said, watching for her reaction.

"I know, that's what I want," she told him.

Whatever he'd expected her to say, it definitely wasn't that.

"What?" he asked dumbly.

Beth looked out at the ocean, then turned back to him, smiling. "I want you to be my first Jeremy. It only makes sense, it has to be you," she said with such calm, and such certainty, that he began feeling like a kid talking to a woman. She bit her lip, looking nervous.

All the love that he felt for her was in his face, reflected by the moonlight. He hid nothing. "Come here," he said, holding out his hand to her. She took it, and he brought her next to him. They sat side by side, looking at the moon. She rested her head on his shoulder, and he stroked her hair.

"Not here, not like this," he whispered, glancing down at her. He had to hide his smile. Her face could not have looked more disappointed.

"I had a really nice time tonight," Rachel said shyly as they sat in Corey's Volkswagon bus.

Corey turned to her with a boyish grin, "Me too. I was afraid you weren't going to like the band."

"No, they were great!" Rachel assured him, and she meant it.

She was a bit nervous when he told her they were going to hear a band play outside a surf shop. She knew the local shops would sometimes throw a party, especially when they were having a big sale, but she never had any interest in going. Of course, she hadn't told Corey that, and had put on her happy game face, hoping the night wouldn't be too awful. Surprisingly, she loved it. The band was great, the people were cool and they had actually danced together....well, more like jumped up and down banging into each other. But it had been fun, really fun.

"Sorry about the food," he said.

"Please, don't worry about it. I told you, I had already eaten before you picked me up," she lied. The only food at the event had been pizza or hot dogs, and she would have rather swam in the ocean than eaten either of those. She had chugged diet soda and water all night.

"Well, I promise to have better food at my party tomorrow night. You guys are coming, right?" he asked. Corey, just like everyone else in their school, knew the four girls were a package deal.

"Totally, can't wait!" she said, and found she truly meant it. "Well, I better go in. Thanks again." She turned to open the door, but he put his hand on her arm.

"Wait," he said quietly, and she turned back to him. He leaned over, and kissed her.

At first, she felt like a deer caught in the headlights. She had only kissed two boys, and that was when she was fourteen. It hadn't occurred to her that Corey would want a goodnight kiss.

He gently moved his mouth over hers, forcing her lips to relax. Once they did, his kiss became more insistent. She found herself clinging to him, kissing him back with newly awakened desire.

Slowly, the kiss ended, and Rachel realized she had somehow ended up in his lap.

"Umm," she mumbled, cheeks burning. She had basically attacked him in her awkwardness. She was mortified. Glancing up, she caught her breath.

He was looking at her with an expression that was anything but amused. His hazel eyes bore into her pale blue ones with an intensity that was almost searing.

"Rachel..honey...wow," he murmered.

"Yeah," she breathed, relieved that he had a similar experience from their kiss.

She was still smiling as she entered her house and leaned against the door. Reality hit when she heard the sounds coming from the back. Quietly she walked through the dark house, and peered out the window. There, in the pool, was her mother and the firefighter. They were both obviously drunk, and naked. If her mother had even remembered Rachel was on a date, she had certainly forgotten by now. Rachel walked into her room and closed the door.

Six

Parrots squawking brought Beth out of a nice, deep slumber. She rolled onto her back, stretched her arms above her head, and smiled. Her night with Jeremy had been wonderful, magical. She reflected back to their time on the beach, and bit her lip in embarrassment. She had practically thrown herself at him! She was sure she had surprised him with her behavior, but no more than she had surprised herself.

She thought on that a moment. Never had she actually wanted a boy before. And she definitely wanted him. The fact that he was the one to slow them down last night would have been humiliating with any other boy. But not with Jeremy, she trusted him, she felt secure with him. He knew her better than anyone, and yet, she didn't feel too comfortable with him. She still cared what he thought, she still wanted to look good for him, impress him. She was attracted to her best friend, what more could a girl ask for?

She was pondering this as she walked past her mom in the hallway, not seeing her. Mary looked at her with a knowing smile and said, "If that smile is any indication, I take it you enjoyed yourself last night?"

Beth turned to her, "What?"

"Nothing," Mary said, laughing to herself as she headed downstairs.

Beth went into the bathroom, and got out the scale. Hesitantly, she stepped on. She was down another pound! She couldn't believe it! She was sure her dinner with Jeremy had screwed things up.

Although, she had appeared to eat more than she actually did. She would have to remember the tricks she used last night when eating with her mom and brother. They worked great! She hopped down the stairs, buoyed by a ridiculous amount of happiness. She had gone on a great date, and found a way to get through dinners with her mom!

She found her mom sitting at the table, reading the paper with a cup of coffee. Billy was sprawled across the family room floor, watching Saturday morning cartoons.

She opened the fridge, looked around and asked, "Mom, where are all the grapefruits?"

"I need to go grocery shopping, I'll get some today," Mary replied.

Beth stared at the fridge, as panic started to creep up. What was she going to eat? She opened all the fruits and veggie bins, finding them empty. Frantically, she scanned the shelves. She almost jumped out of her skin when her mom said behind her, "Why don't you have some yogurt?"

Beth looked at the yogurt. It wasn't the most ideal choice, as it was loaded with sugar, and had three grams of fat, but it was the lowest caloric choice. She would just have to make up for it later. She grabbed the yogurt and sat down with a sigh.

"Soooo, how was it?" Mary asked with a smile.

Beth couldn't help but smile back. "It was nice. It was...perfect actually."

Her mom's smile grew wider. "Good. You know I've loved Jeremy since he was a little boy. I definitely approve of the young man he's become," she finished as she washed out her coffee cup.

"We're going to a party tonight, at Corey Lasalle's," she told her mother. "I mean, Rachel, Jenny, Melanie and me," she corrected. "But, Jeremy will be there, of course."

"Are Corey's parents going to be home?" Mary asked pointedly.

"Yeah, don't worry, we are going to hang out downstairs," Beth told her as she finished her yogurt and water. She noticed her mom staring at the yogurt, and got up quickly to rinse out the container for recycling. She knew what was coming.

"Is that all you're eating?"

"Yeah, you know I don't eat that much in the morning," she said, concentrating so hard on rinsing the yogurt cup that it took her a minute before she realized she had started actually washing the container, with dish soap. She opened the cabinet door and threw the container in the small recycling bin her mother kept under the sink. She knew her mom was watching her.

"Actually, you've always eaten quite a big breakfast, huge sometimes. I couldn't keep enough waffles in the house!"

"That was when I was little," Beth said, trying to laugh off the conversation.

"No," Mary stated as she got up from the kitchen table. "That was a few months ago."

She turned to her mom. "Well, a lot has changed over the last few months, hasn't it? Maybe I've lost some of my appetite."

Mary looked down. "I know. I'm sorry Beth."

Immediately, Beth regretted her words. "Mom, it's not your fault! He left, you didn't throw him out."

Mary smiled sadly. "You know, sometimes I'm not sure what happened, exactly."

Beth glanced at Billy, who had stopped watching his cartoons, and was listening to their exchange. She looked back at her mother, "I think we all feel that way."

Mary nodded. "Okay, but please, please make sure you're eating enough, and I'll lay off. Deal?"

She hugged her mom. "Deal."

Mary left to run errands, and Beth plopped down on the couch to watch tv.

"Billy, can't we watch something else besides SpongeBob?" she asked her brother.

"No," was all he said.

She knew those were fighting words, but she was too tired to argue. Her energy level was usually at it's highest in the morning, and she wondered if she was coming down with something. SpongeBob wasn't the worst thing to watch, she conceded, drifting off into veg land. They were into their third episode when her cell rang.

"Hello," she said into the phone, distracted by the cartoon show.

"Hey! How was your night?" Melanie's excited voice asked.

Beth got off the couch and walked out the slider to the back patio. She sat in a lounge chair by the pool and spent the next hour describing her date in detail. She thought Melanie was going to pee her pants by the time she hung up. The sun felt good to her bones, and she laid her head back to soak it up. The ringing of her phone woke her with a start.

"Hello?" she said, slightly disoriented.

"Okay, I'm dying to know, how'd it go?" Jenny asked, all business. Beth smiled and relayed her entire night to Jenny's attentive ears.

"Wow B. I mean, Wow!" Jenny said toward the end of their conversation.

"I know," she said. She hung up with Jenny and looked around, wondering what time it was. She couldn't believe she had fallen asleep, only a few hours after waking up! She went inside to work on her report for English.

By one o' clock, the growling of her tummy became something she couldn't continue to ignore. As usual, she checked her email for a response from her father. There wasn't one, so she logged off and went downstairs in search of a minimalist meal. Her mom had returned, only to leave again to take Billy to football practice, so at least she would be able to eat, or not eat, in peace. Mary had definitely gone food shopping, the fridge and cupboards were full!

She searched, trying to find something with very little, or no calories. It occurred to Beth that it was much easier to diet during the week, when she had the structure and routine of school and activities to not only keep her distracted from her hunger, but keep her on track in general. She began to feel anxious as she searched and searched for something acceptable to eat.

Finally, she found a Lean Cuisine in the freezer, left over from when her mom was on Weight Watchers during the summer. She checked the calories and the date on the box. Finding both acceptable, she popped it in the microwave. As it cooked, the smell of food made her mouth water so much that she almost choked. All she could do was stare at the microwave, counting down the minutes, then seconds, until it was done.

Spoon in hand, she grabbed it a second before the beep went off. Not bothering to sit at the table, she stood in the middle of the kitchen, scooping food into her mouth. Nothing had ever tasted so good! She didn't even mind that the outer edges were so hot they burned her tongue, and the very middle was still a little frozen.

Finished, she stared at the empty container longingly, hoping somehow more food would appear. It didn't, so she threw it away. Then something strange happened. She was hungrier now than she was before she ate.

"What the hell?" she muttered to herself. Slowly, she opened the fridge, and found that everything, absolutely everything, looked good. She scanned the shelves a few times, looking at each piece of food as if it were a rare jewel, becoming almost hypnotized by it. She slammed the door shut.

"Hey Beth!" Jeremy yelled as he came out his front door.

"Hey Jeremy," she replied. She had thrown on her running gear, tied her hair up, and gotten out of the house. A good run would take care of everything.

"Going for a run?" he asked, walking toward her.

"Yeah," she said, feeling a little shy. Images from the night before flashed in her mind, and she found herself looking at her feet as he walked up.

"I just wanted to tell you...." He began, then realized she wasn't going to look back up at him. He put his finger under her chin, gently applying pressure. Tentatively, she raised her gaze to his. "Your not going to turn shy on me now, are you?" he asked, teasing.

Beth felt her cheeks warm at his knowing gaze. He continued, "I just wanted to tell you, I had a great time last night."

She smiled, one of the sweetest smiles he thought he had ever seen. "Me too, thank you again."

They stood like that, neither one willing to break contact. He still had his finger under her chin, so he decided the next logical step was to kiss her. He'd wanted to kiss her again from the moment he'd said goodnight to her. He leaned his head down, capturing her lips in a swift kiss. "I'll see you tonight at Corey's, right?" he murmured once their lips parted.

"Yes," she whispered. Then she cleared her throat. "I'm gonna go run now," she said, smiling.

"By all means m'lady!" he yelled after her as she ran down the street.

Saturday had been pizza night since the day Beth was born. The four of them would sit at the kitchen table, playing board games and eating pizza. Her parents would drink a few beers, and the kids would get soda, a once a week treat. As a little girl, she had always looked forward to Saturday because of pizza night.

After her parents divorce, her mother had continued the tradition. Beth assumed it was her way of trying to keep things consistent and normal for her kids. For Beth, it accomplished the opposite. She dreaded pizza night, mainly due to the fact that every Saturday night, as she sat with her mom and brother, she felt her father's absence more than ever. She was grateful her mom didn't insist they play a board game!

She looked at her mother as the three of them sat at the kitchen table, eating their pizza. Mary Baxter was still pretty, very pretty actually. She always had a kind and giving heart. She also had a stubborn streak, Beth thought to herself, smiling. She was sure the determination that came naturally to her mother had sustained her through the painful betrayal of her husband. There had been times Beth had listened through her mother's bedroom door, and heard her crying. Even Billy, who seemed oblivious to almost everything, became instantly protective of their mother when their dad left.

Beth glanced at him. At ten years old, Billy was your typical boy. His blond hair was too long, causing him to shove it out of his eyes constantly. He had their mother's blue eyes, which she was sure would be a great asset to him once he reached his teen years. Overall, she conceded, he was a great looking kid, taking after their mother in looks.

Beth had gotten her father's dark hair, brown eyes and olive skin. She pushed any thoughts of her father away, and looked down at the piece of cheese pizza her mom had dropped on her plate. She had managed to eat about half, feeling guilty with every bite.

"So, who's driving tonight?" Mary asked, biting into her second piece of pizza.

"Melanie. She's so excited to drive her new car," Beth said, trying to get down another bite of pizza. "What are you guys doing tonight?"

"Connor's comin' over," Billy mumbled as he grabbed a piece of pizza, his third.

"Oh, cool," she said, looking at her mom.

"Yeah, I have an exciting night of listening to the two of them play video games," Mary laughed, smiling at Billy.

Just then someone knocked. Beth hurried to answer the door, relieved to have a diversion that would get her out of finishing her pizza.

"Hey!" Melanie said excitedly. "Ready?"

"Yeah, I just need to grab my purse," she said, running upstairs. She checked her appearance one more time in the mirror, and smiled with satisfaction. She wore a pair of vintage cut-offs with a purple and white batiked shirt that accented her tan nicely. She slipped her feet into a pair of black Reef flip-flops, and reached for her brush.

"I thought you just had to grab your purse B!" Melanie called from the bottom of the stairs. "She never used to take so long to get ready!" she said to Mrs. Baxter.

Mary glanced up the stairs, then back at Melanie with a smile. "Well, that was before she finally noticed the nice looking young man who's been living across the street from her for the past sixteen years." They both laughed.

"What's so funny?" Beth asked, bounding down the stairs.

"Nothing," they said in unison, still smiling at each other.

"Yeah, right," she said. "Ready?"

"I was the one waiting, remember?" Melanie said, shoving her out the door.

"Have fun! Be safe girls!" Mary yelled, waving.

She shut the door, and headed back to the kitchen to clean up. Grabbing the paper plates off the table, she frowned at Beth's half-eaten slice of pizza.

"I've got the worst headache!" Beth said, throwing two Advil in her mouth and washing it down with her ever present bottle of water.

"How much are you eating?" Melanie asked worriedly.

"Enough. It's just hard, because I'm thinking about food all of the time now. It's so weird, I never used to be like that, you know?"

Melanie nodded. She understood exactly what Beth meant. Food wasn't an issue for Melanie, it never had been. She ate when she was hungry, and that was that. She tried to eat enough fruits and vegetables, and not pig out on the sweets, and exercise. She assumed she was able to keep weight off because she had always played sports.

"Maybe your body is telling you that you aren't eating enough," she suggested.

Beth thought for a moment. "Maybe...but it's hard to give in to eating more when I'm seeing the results come so quickly. I mean, look at me, even I have to admit I'm rockin' these cut-offs!"

Both girls burst into laughter.

"At least you're still humble about it!" Melanie laughed.

"You know what I mean! These shorts used to be tight, now they fit perfect. I accomplished that in less than a week! Imagine what I'll look like by the end of the month!"

That was what Melanie was worried about, but she decided to drop it. Tonight was for fun, not lecturing.

They swung into Jenny's driveway. The front door opened before they even got out of the car, and Jenny came running toward them.

"Let's go!" she said as she climbed in the back. "Where have you guys been? I've been waiting for like ten minutes!"

Melanie and Beth looked at each other. Jenny wasn't known for her patience. Five minutes later they were at Rachel's. She was standing at the end of her driveway, waiting for them.

"How long were you standing out there?" Melanie asked.

"Since you texted me," Rachel told her.

"I told you I'd be a half hour!"

"I know. I couldn't sit in there with them. They're starting to get drunk and the jerk's friend is over."

"Oh," was all Melanie said.

"Hey, turn it up, I love this song," Rachel told her, eager to change the subject.

"Oh my God," Jenny muttered as they passed dozens of cars parked in the street outside Corey's house. "There is no way his folks are home!"

Beth was thinking the exact same thing. She was also thinking about what she had told her mom. "Mel, park just around the corner."

"Got it," Melanie said, already understanding.

"What? I don't want to walk a mile to get to the party!" Jenny complained.

"Jen, if the cops bust the party, we can make a run for the car and get out of here. If we park too close they will either see us trying to leave, or have our car blocked in," Rachel calmly explained.

"Oh, right..." Jenny said. "Good thinkin'!"

"Nervous?" Beth asked, watching Rachel touch up her lip gloss. Immediately she stopped, shoved the lip gloss back in her purse and looked at Beth innocently.

They could hear the thump-thump sounds of music coming from inside as they approached the door. Melanie opened it, and the music blasted them in the face. They walked through the maze of kids, looking for Corey. Not finding him, they headed out back. Kids were strewn everywhere, in chairs, leaning against trees, lying on the ground, a few were even in the pool. Some were making out, some were talking, a few were getting stoned.

Even though Rachel knew most of the kids, she always felt like a fish out of water around them. She glanced down at her outfit, comparing it to what the other girls had on, and felt a little better. The weight Rachel had dropped made her jeans fit even better, and her black halter top fit perfectly, except in the bust. About two years ago Rachel had found peace with the fact that she would probably never get past her A, almost B cup. It was something she had become grateful for as her mother's boyfriends began to show more interest. She ran her hands through her shoulder length black hair and looked around. "I don't see him," she told the others. "Let's go get a drink."

They found the keg, paid for a cup, and filled up.

"I think they're playing drinking games on the deck," Jenny said excitedly.

She was right. A group of about ten kids were sitting around a table, playing quarters. One of them was Corey, and Rachel's stomach fell to her knees when she saw him. His blond hair was hanging everywhere and she thought he couldn't have looked more adorable. He glanced at her, looked away, then looked back again, his face instantly lighting up.

"Rachel!" he exclaimed as he removed himself from the group. "I was wondering when you were going to get here."

Rachel, who had stood frozen in place from the moment she first saw him, actually blushed. Beth couldn't remember a time when she had ever seen Rachel blush.

"We, um, got some beer," Rachel said, waving her cup around as she talked. Some of the contents splashed out, landing on Corey's toes. "Oh! Sorry…" she muttered, embarrassed.

He just laughed, put his arm around her and turned to the other girls. "Rachel and I are gonna go hang," he told them over his shoulder as he led her toward the pool. The girls watched them walk over to a pair of lounge chairs and sit down.

"Well, I guess we won't be seeing her again tonight," Melanie mumbled, sighing. They walked back in the house, ending up in the kitchen.

"Hey girls!" a tanned, handsome boy hollered to them from across the kitchen. "Wanna shot?" He held up a shot glass filled with yellow liquid, rimmed with sugar.

"Sure!" Jenny said as they walked over. The boy smiled and handed the shot glass to her. She glanced at the other two girls, who were watching her intently, and drank the shot in one gulp. "Wow! Yum!" she exclaimed. "Thanks," she said to the boy, smiling. He smiled right back, and filled up another shot.

"My name's Brian, I'm Corey's cousin. What's your names?" he asked the three of them.

Jenny handled the introductions, and Brian handed each girl a shot, then grabbed one for himself. "It's nice to meet you girls," he said, but was staring straight at Jenny. Melanie and Beth looked at each other, rolling their eyes. Jenny just kept smiling at Brian.

"Dammit!" Jeremy muttered as he began his second attempt to parallel park near Corey's house. He had meant to get to the party over an hour ago, but baseball practice ran late and his grandparents had come over for dinner. He was sure Beth was already inside. His eagerness to see her surprised him. Besides running two red lights, he had screamed and cursed out the car in front of him for driving too slow. He was shocked when he finally passed the car and realized it was an elderly couple, but no more shocked than them. "Finally!" he muttered, and jumped out of the car.

"Hey Jeremy," a blond girl from his science lab purred when he entered the house. She threw her arms around him and drunkenly whispered, "When are we gonna get together?"

Jeremy gently pulled her arms from around his neck, leaving the disappointed girl with her friends. He wandered through the crowd, yelling over the music, asking people if they'd seen Beth. Someone pointed in the direction of the kitchen.

He entered the noisy kitchen and it took him a minute to digest what he was seeing. Beth and Jenny were standing on the island in the middle of the kitchen. They danced to the music while a group of guys cheered from below. Jeremy folded his arms over his chest, and leaned against the kitchen counter, watching. He had to admit, the girls did have some great moves. One of the guys handed Beth a shot of something, which she drank down quickly. He wondered how many of those shots she'd accepted.

"Hey Jeremy!" a familiar voice said. He looked over to see Melanie smiling up at him, beer cup in hand.

"Hey Mel, what's goin' on?" he asked, gesturing to the dancing girls.

Melanie looked in their direction, and smiled. "Oh you know, they're having fun! I can't drink like that tonight, I'm driving," she explained.

"I can see that," he said, looking at her cup meaningfully. Melanie followed his gaze.

"Oh no, this is diet Pepsi, see," she said, holding it up for him to sniff. He leaned down, and smelled soda. "I had a couple sips of beer, and one shot."

Jeremy nodded, turning his attention back to the girls. One of the guys reached up and rubbed Beth's leg. She swatted his hand away and yelled something at him. He laughed and reached up again, rubbing further up this time.

Before he knew what he was doing, Jeremy launched through the crowd and grabbed the guy.

"Don't touch her!" he yelled over the music. Whatever the other guy saw in Jeremy's eyes made him put up his hands in surrender.

"Sorry dude, didn't know she was taken," he yelled back.

Frustrated with his lack of self control, Jeremy looked up at Beth, who was looking at him in shock. He reached up and grabbed her hand, pulling her into his arms.

"What are you doin'?" she slurred, and he found himself even more angry realizing she was drunk.

"Taking you out to get some air!" he said in that voice she hated.

She wiggled out of his arms and yelled, "Put me down!" Then she ran ahead of him.

He calmly followed her, because she was heading in the right direction. He caught up with her on the deck, catching her just before she would escape him.

"Beth, wait!" he said, grabbing her around the waist. "Where are you going?"

She stopped struggling. "I don't know," she said quietly.

He smiled to himself. "Listen, let's go find a place to sit down, okay?" he said, slowly releasing her. As soon as he did, she began to sway. "Shit, how much did you drink?"

"I don't know," she said again, her voice shaking.

He realized she couldn't stand up on her own. If he picked her up and carried her to a chair, it would cause a scene. "Okay, put your arm around my neck, like this...good...now lean into me like you are going to kiss me...good," he said roughly, as her lips accidentally touched his. "We are going to walk over to the chairs on the grass, while we're making out.

Her eyes opened wide. "What?" she began to say, just as his lips captured hers.

Somehow, he guided them to the chairs. To onlookers, they looked like a drunken couple that needed a room, which was exactly what Jeremy wanted them to think. Gently, he settled her into a lounge chair, and started to sit in the one beside it. She caught his hand, saying, "Sit with me."

Never one to disappoint, he sank down next to her. He wrapped his arms around her, and she snuggled right in, fitting perfectly.

She tried to focus on the tree above them, and saw little lights sparkling on the branches.

"Why does Corey have Christmas lights up already?" she slurred.

Jeremy glanced up. "Those are stars," he said quietly, kissing her forehead.

"Oh...they're really pretty," she said. All of a sudden the stars started moving, spinning in a circle above her head. Her stomach gave a lurch, and she shot off the chair, covering her mouth.

"Okay, okay," he said, quickly guiding her behind the tree. He caught her hair a split second before she wretched. "It's alright," he soothed, rubbing her back. She threw up over and over, until she was dry heaving.

"Is she okay?" someone asked. He turned his head to see Rachel and Corey standing behind him.

"Yeah, she just needs some water."

"I threw some in the cooler on the deck, just in case," Corey said.

"How much did she drink?" Jeremy asked Rachel after Corey left to fetch the water.

Rachel shrugged her shoulders and said, "I honestly don't know, I've been out here with Corey."

"I'm okay, I'm okay," Beth panted. Slowly, she stood up and leaned against the tree. "Thank you," she said, looking at Jeremy. Then she began to collapse. He caught her and set her down in the

lounge chair.   Corey ran up and handed him the
water bottle.

"Beth, drink some of this," he said softly,
holding her head up. After a few gulps, she leaned
against the chair, looking exhausted. A thought
occurred to him.

"How much did she have to eat today?" he
asked Rachel.

Rachel looked everywhere but at Jeremy.
"Um, I don't know, we didn't talk about it."

"Bullshit Rachel! I have a feeling that's all
you guys have been talking about lately!" he said,
disgusted.

Corey looked at Rachel. "What's he talking
about?"

Rachel smiled at him, "Nothing, nothing. We
started a stupid diet, you know, to lose a few
pounds."

Corey straightened, and looked her up and
down from the top of her head to her last pinky toe.
By the time he was done, Rachel was sure her
cheeks were as red as a tomato.

"You know you're hot, right?" he asked with a
concerned look on his face.   His flippant words
combined with genuine concern was so sweet and
pure, it made her want to cry. Instead, she focused
her attention back to Jeremy, hoping her own
vulnerability wasn't showing too much on her face.

"You're right, we talk weight and food...what
girls don't? But, I didn't see her until tonight. We
were so excited about the party that none of us
talked about it," she told him, realizing it for the
first time herself.

Considering Corey was the "host" of tonight's fun, she had wanted to be at her best for him. Coming down with another headache, or suffering bouts of dizziness, wouldn't have helped. As a result, she had eaten an entire bowl of healthy cereal with a generous amount of soymilk. By the time she finished the last bite, her stomach felt like it was going to burst. She was grateful for the food though, her night with Corey had been awesome so far.

She surmised that Beth hadn't eaten much of anything in preparation of the night ahead, and was suffering for it.

"Corey, let's go make some toast, it will help settle Beth's stomach," she said, already pulling him with her towards the house.

"Yeah, okay, we'll be right back Jer," Corey said over his shoulder.

"Thanks," Jeremy yelled after them, then turned his attention back to Beth. She was staring back at him. "Why are you doing this?" he asked her.

She was too tired and too drunk to play games. "Just wanna be...different person," she mumbled.

He shook his head and helped her drink more water. "Beth," he began, taking a deep breath, "there aren't enough words to describe how special you are."

She smiled weakly, and placed her hand on his cheek. "You are so sweet, always have been."

"It has nothing to do with being sweet," he said forcefully. "I-" he began, then stopped. He didn't want her to be drunk the first time he told her that he loved her.

She kept staring at him, smiling, which proved just how out of it she was. A sober Beth would have insisted he tell her what he was about to say. "Hey, make some room for me, will ya?" he joked, stretching out next to her. Once again she snuggled into his shoulder.

"Excuse me!" Rachel shouted over the music. A couple was leaning against the fridge door, blocking her from getting to the bread. "Hey guys, move!" she yelled again, this time shoving the boy's shoulder. They looked at her, and moved over just enough so she could open the door. "Thanks," she said sarcastically.

She grabbed the bread and pushed her way through the throngs of people to get to the other side of the kitchen where Corey waited. "Here," she said, tossing him the bread.

He threw in two slices and turned back to her. Someone pushed into her back, causing her to fall right into his arms. "Sorry," she mumbled, trying to steady herself.

Corey tightened his hold on her. "It's cool," he said in her ear and kissed her.

Rachel had never kissed anyone in public before. With Corey, she didn't care who was watching.

"Dude! Your toast!" one of Corey's friends yelled to them.

Slowly he withdrew his mouth from hers and smiled sheepishly. "The toast," he murmured.

She nodded and threw the toast in a paper towel. Grabbing her hand, Corey led them out of the house. They found Jeremy and Beth wrapped in each other's arms, asleep. Quietly Corey leaned down and set the wrapped toast next to them on the chair. He looked at Rachel and put his finger to his mouth. She stifled a giggle as they tiptoed away.

An hour later, Beth opened her eyes. She tilted her head up and felt the roughness of whiskers rub against her forehead. She studied the profile of the young man she was practically laying on top of, and smiled. In slumber, Jeremy resembled more of the boy she grew up with than the man he was becoming.

He sensed her looking at him, and turned his head. "How ya feelin'?" he asked, his voice thick from sleep.

"Better," she croaked, then winced. Her throat felt like it was on fire. "Do you have any water?"

"Yeah," he said, searching for the bottle. Handing it to her, he watched her chug down the rest. "Easy, you might get sick again."

She stopped drinking and sat up, ready for the pain she knew would hit her. Not feeling any, she looked down at him, surprised. "My head doesn't hurt!"

"Probably because you threw up, got it outta ya," he said, studying her. "How much did you drink?"

She thought back. "I had a cup of beer, and three lemon shots. I don't know why I got so drunk, or so sick. I've drank more than that and not gotten nearly as wasted."

"How much did you eat today?" he asked quietly. Beth's eyes darted to his knowing ones, and looked away. "That's what I thought," he said, sitting up next to her. "Can you stand?"

"I think so," she said, pushing herself up. She swayed a bit, but quickly found her balance. "Where are the girls?" she asked, looking around.

"Rachel and Corey have been glued to each other's sides all night, and the last time I saw Mel and Jen, they were in the kitchen." Out of the corner of his eye, he saw something on the chair. "Here," he said, pushing a piece of toast at her. She began to argue, and he said, "You're kidding, right?"

Reluctantly she grabbed it out of his hand and began chewing the dry bread. Halfway through the first piece, her stomach started to settle. Jeremy stood with his arms crossed over his chest, watching her chew each piece. She looked everywhere but at him as she ate. By the time she was into the second piece, her stomach felt normal again and very full.

"I can't eat anymore," she said, handing it to him.

Jeremy peered at her, then took the bread. He broke it into pieces and threw it on the grass for the egrets to eat in the morning.

"You wanna go inside?" he asked.

Beth smoothed her hair and ran her fingers under her eyes, trying to remove any mascara that may have smudged. "How do I look?" she asked, looking up at him expectantly.

Jeremy looked into her big brown eyes and found himself lost. "Beautiful," he stated flatly.

She smiled, leaned up on her tip-toes and kissed him. Just as she was about to pull away, he wrapped his arms around her and crushed her body to him. Minutes later, they were breathless, and Jeremy's desire for her threatened his ability to have rational thought. He focused on anything except the girl walking next to him as they headed back toward the house.

They found Jenny in a heated game of quarters. Brian, Corey's cousin, was sitting next to her. Beth guessed he hadn't left her side all night. Her assumption was confirmed minutes later as Jenny leaned over and kissed Brian, who kissed her right back.

"Hey guys!" Melanie yelled from a corner of the deck. Dylan Scott, captain of the basketball team, was standing next to her.

Melanie had a crush on Dylan since the sixth grade. Silently and patiently, she had remained his friend while he dated his way through their school. With her usual confidence, she waited, knowing one day Dylan would wake up and finally see what was standing right in front of him. By the way Dylan couldn't keep his eyes off her, it seemed that day had finally arrived.

"Are you okay? I heard you got sick," she said to Beth, scanning her face worriedly. "I was going to look for you, but Rachel said you were in good hands." She smiled at Jeremy.

"I can see you are as well," Beth whispered to Melanie, who giggled. "How many people know I got sick?" she asked.

"Not too many, right Dylan?" she asked, looking at the handsome junior. He looked back with such adoration on his face that Beth almost wept with happiness for her friend. Melanie might have been tolerant of Dylan all these years, but Beth had continued to become more frustrated with him. She was happy to see her friend was finally getting her due.

"Right, no one knows," he said to Melanie, then belatedly turned to Beth and nodded.

"Are you okay?" Melanie asked again.

"Yeah, I was well taken care of," Beth said, grabbing Jeremy's hand.

Melanie nodded, "I'm sure you were," she said, smiling. She glanced at her watch. "My curfew's up in fifteen minutes. We have to go," she said, glancing at Dylan.

"Um, Mel, can I have your cell number?" Dylan asked eagerly.

Melanie gave him her biggest smile, and it took Dylan a moment to realize she had nodded and was starting to recite her number.

"Wait, hold on," he said, grabbing his phone out of his pocket. "Okay, tell me again." He kissed Melanie on the cheek and told them all goodnight.

Melanie rubbed her cheek, smiling.

"I'll take Beth home," Jeremy blurted, pulling Melanie out of her trance. Realizing he hadn't even bothered to ask Beth, he said with a half smile, "Um, if that's okay with you."

She smiled back, "Sounds good."

"I'm gonna text Rachel," Melanie said. "Wow, she's staying here tonight, with Corey!" she exclaimed, looking at Beth and Jeremy. "She said her mom won't notice whether she comes home or not."

"She's right," Beth mumbled, "That woman doesn't notice anything other than herself."

Melanie nodded in agreement, and sighed. "Well, now I just need to get Jenny away from Corey's cousin!"

She walked around the table and whispered into Jenny's ear, which resulted in Jenny looking longingly at Brian. They exchanged cell numbers and shared one more kiss before Melanie practically pulled Jenny out of her chair and dragged her into the house, leaving Brian looking a bit forlorn.

"See you guys!" she yelled over her shoulder.

"See ya!" Jeremy yelled back, then turned to Beth. "Wanna go to the beach?" he murmured, and there was no mistaking the look in his eyes.

"I can't, it's almost time for my curfew too!" she said, looking very disappointed.

"Oh," he replied, equally disappointed.

"I wanted a little more time with you, even if it's just a car ride home," she admitted shyly.

Jeremy looked at her, wanting to reach for her, wanting to kiss her senseless. Instead, he grabbed two bottles of water out of the cooler and led her out the side gate.

"Are you sure you're gonna be okay?" he asked as they stood in his driveway.

"I'm good, thank you for taking care of me tonight. I hope I didn't ruin the party for you," she said.

"You're the only reason I wanted to go," he replied, surprising himself with the admission. Never had he told a girl so much about what he was thinking and feeling. He realized he enjoyed this newfound part of himself, and attributed the discovery to his friendship with her. He wondered what other new aspects of this relationship he would experience as a result of being friends with her for most of his life. He had never been friends with a girl before dating her, and had always thought more about making out than really knowing her.

"I wanted to see you too," she said quietly, and Jeremy did what he'd wanted to do all night. He pulled her into his arms and covered her mouth with his.

Seven

"Beth...Beth," Mary's voice called, awakening her out of a great dream. She rolled over and put her pillow over her head.

"Not yet Mom, I want to sleep in!" she moaned.

"Honey, you did sleep in. It's ten o' clock!" Mary exclaimed, standing by the bed. "I take it you had a great time last night?"

"Yeah, it was fun. Jeremy brought me home."

"I know, I looked out the window when I heard his car and saw the two of you in his driveway...Don't worry, I didn't see anything!" she said when Beth rolled over, pinning her with a look. "Since I knew you were home safe, I went to bed, promise."

Beth smiled dreamily, thinking of the kiss they had shared.

"Your dad called, I told him you'd call back once you were up," she said, leaving the room.

Beth sat up, and the room spun a bit. She walked to the bathroom a little more slowly than usual. She stood on the scale, not expecting much. She couldn't believe it, she had lost another pound. That brought her weight to 115 pounds. She had lost a total of five pounds in less than a week! No wonder her clothes were fitting more loosely.

She left the bathroom more motivated than ever to get to her goal weight of 110 pounds. Then she would be as thin as Christine. She would feel just as beautiful too, she was sure of it! She bounded down the stairs, smiling happily as she entered the kitchen. She ate her grapefruit while watching her mom plant flowers out back.

"He's not coming you know," her brother said from the family room.

She turned towards him, "What?"

"Dad's not coming today," Billy repeated, not looking away from the television.

"What are you talking about? Of course he's coming, he promised," she said.

"I heard mom arguing with him on the phone," he said. Then he looked at her, only for a second, but she saw it in his eyes. He was trying not to cry.

She looked back at her mom, watching her attack the soil with her shovel. Throughout the years, whenever her parents had an argument, her mother had always ended up outside, planting something. There were times when their backyard looked eligible for one of those Home and Garden Shows. During the months leading up to the divorce, her mother had moved from the backyard to the front, earning her family the "Best Yard of the Neighborhood" award three months in a row.

Beth got up from the table, threw out her grapefruit and ran upstairs to call her father.

"Hello?"

"Hey Dad, what's up?" she asked, trying to stay calm, trying to give him the benefit of the doubt.

"Hey sweetheart! How are you?" he asked.

"Good, everything's good."

"How's sophomore year going?"

"Good...lots of homework, you know.."

"Yeah...So,"

"What time are you picking us up?" she asked, interrupting him.

"Well, about that honey...I'm not going to be able to pick you and your brother up today."

"Why not?" she asked, already knowing the answer would have something to do with Samantha. She was correct.

"Well, Samantha's niece is turning eight and the party is today, and well, I need to go."

She closed her eyes, and took a deep breath.

"Honey, are you still there?"

"Yeah."

"Listen, I will make it up to you guys. Next week, we'll do something really special, I promise."

"That's what you said last Sunday, Dad," she said, keeping her voice calm. She wanted to scream at him.

"I know...I know, but I promise, next week, we're on, okay honey?"

"Sure Dad. I gotta go."

"Okay, I'll talk to you towards the end of the week."

"Okay, bye."

She hung up the phone and looked around her room. She looked at the beautiful white furniture she had picked out on a shopping trip with her dad. The walls he had painted soft lavender, the color she had picked out at the paint store. The small jewelry boxes he would buy for her from every country he traveled to on business.

She looked at the framed photo on her desk. It was a picture from a trip they had taken to Disney World when she was eleven and Billy was five. Her dad had asked Cinderella to take a photo of them, and at the last minute, Prince Charming made bunny ears over the princess's pretty head. They were all laughing in the picture.

Beth wanted to go back to that day. Go back to before. Before he started working late. Before he increased his business trips. Before he started having an affair. Before he left them.

There were times she looked at it like someone else's life. One day, they were a happy family going to Disney World together. The next, he was packing his things. Packing all of the familiar things that Beth grew up around. His golf bag, his clothes, his books, his cologne, his fishing poles....

He had left her and Billy's poles behind, which had hurt more than if he would have taken them. They hadn't been touched since he left, with promises that he would still take them fishing. Their poles leaned against the garage wall, alone. The garage was an empty place now. It used to be filled with her father's tools and projects, with his surfboard and his bike. He took it all with him, literally leaving them with only memories. And although she finally felt comfortable in the house again, she knew it would never be the home she grew up in.

"Is he coming?" Billy asked from her doorway.

Beth looked at him. "No."

"Why not?" he asked resentfully.

"He has to go to some stupid thing for Samantha's family. He said we'll do something next week."

"Yeah right," he said, and walked into his room, shutting the door. A minute later she heard music blasting.

She didn't blame him for being mad, she was furious! Samantha was taking more and more time away from them with her demands. Beth felt the usual hatred that always surfaced when she thought of the woman her father had left them for.

At thirty, she was fourteen years his junior. She was tall, thin and had big fake boobs...she was a walking cliché. Beth's father was a salesman for a large software company based in their town, and Samantha had been a receptionist that worked there. Noel Baxter was one of the company's most successful sales reps. Beth was sure that as soon as Samantha realized who her dad was, she had set her sights on him. She was also sure that her dad had lost his mind.

It was the only reasonable explanation for the decision making that led him from being a loving and devoted husband and father, to a guy sleeping with the equivalent of a secretary. What hurt and confused Beth the most was that he so easily gave up his life with them, for her. He had become more and more distant from them since the divorce. It left a void inside her that she couldn't even begin to comprehend, let alone actually deal with.

She hadn't talked to anyone about the divorce, not even Jeremy. She had participated in conversations with her mother, mainly to make her mom feel better, as well as letting her think she was really helping Beth. But she had never really talked about it. She still couldn't find the words. The emotions were so raw, and over the last few months they had gotten stronger. There were times Beth didn't know what to do, she felt so much pain inside. Usually she would surf for hours, until her soul was numb. The pain was getting harder and harder to ignore and she didn't know how to handle it. She was almost afraid of it.

Screw it! she thought to herself, and threw on her running gear.

"I'm goin' for a run," she yelled to her mom from the sliding glass door.

Mary leaned back on her heels and looked at Beth. "Did you talk to your father?"

"Yeah, I'm goin' running, okay?"

"Wait, are you okay?" her mother asked, starting to stand up.

"I'm fine, gottta go," she said, shutting the door.

She grabbed her iPod, turned Audioslave up as loud as her ears could stand, and headed out the front door. She had the music so loud that she didn't hear Jeremy call her name from across the street. She took off running, pushing and pushing, running it out, searching for the numb bliss.

She didn't know how long she'd ran, but her mom and brother were gone when she returned. There was a text from her mom saying that she took Billy and his friend to the movies. At least Billy would let their mom do something to make it better.

She paced, feeling the pain coming on. The run hadn't solved her problem. God, what was she going to do? Just then she spotted a box of Hostess cupcakes on the counter, and her stomach growled. She walked over to the box, and tried to stare it down. It stared right back, almost daring her. She grabbed a cupcake out of the box, ripped it open and ate it in two bites. Then she ate another. Frantically, she searched the cupboards, pulling out chips, pretzels, licorice, pudding, everything. She grabbed handfuls and shoved it into her mouth, chewing faster and faster, trying to get it down quickly so she wouldn't have time to think about what she was doing. She moved to the freezer, pulled out the ice cream, and ate spoonful after spoonful straight out of the container. She opened the fridge and grabbed a piece of pizza from the night before, then another one. She ate and ate until she couldn't eat anymore, until she felt like her insides were going to split apart.

"Oh no," she moaned, looking at the destruction she had done. Food was everywhere. She hurried to put it all away, and sat down in a kitchen chair, trying to come to grips with what she'd just done. All of the weight she'd lost, it would come back. All her hard work over the past week would be for nothing!

"Noooo," she wailed, putting her head in her arms. Then she remembered something. She'd heard of girls at school who puked after eating so they wouldn't gain weight. At the time, Beth had thought it was disgusting....now, it sounded like a brilliant idea.

She went upstairs to the bathroom, shut the door, and locked it. Kneeling before the toilet, she stuck her fingers down her throat, and started to gag. Immediately, she pulled her fingers out. Her eyes were watering and she wiped them.

"Okay, I can do this!" Beth said to herself.

She put her fingers down her throat again and pressed on the back of it, holding it down even when her instinct was to stop. She pulled them back out, started heaving, then puked. She recognized almost everything she had eaten. She did it again, and puked again, seeing more food. She did it again, and puked again. This time there was only a little food. She didn't know if she should stop or keep going. Assuming that she had gotten most of it, she decided to stop. Her belly felt empty again, but her throat felt raw. So raw. She blew her nose, threw the paper in the toilet and flushed it all down. Then she stood up, feeling weak. She decided that a long, hot shower would make her feel better.

"Honey, where are you?" Mary called.

"Up here Mom," Beth yelled, her voice hoarse from vomiting. After her shower, she had snuggled into bed and dozed off.

"Naptime?" her mother asked with a sympathetic smile.

"Yeah, just tired from last night."

"Well, it's no wonder, two late nights in a row. She paused. Are you sure you're okay, you know, about your dad?" she asked, concerned.

"Yeah, its fine, I was tired anyway," Beth assured her, pulling the covers higher under her chin.

"Okay, do you want some more water? You sound like you have a frog in your throat!"

"No thanks, I'll drink some when I get up," she said, rolling over. "I'm gonna sleep some more."

Mary closed the door quietly. Beth was grateful that her mother attributed her scratchy voice to sleep. She hoped it would be back to normal by dinner. She woke up two hours later, made some tea for her throat and sat outside in a lounge chair near the pool. Although the typical Florida sun shone down, it wasn't too humid, and there was a nice breeze. The sweet scents from her mother's flowers surrounded her senses, and she took a deep breath, taking it in.

Mary stuck her head out the door. "Beth, Jeremy's at the door, are you up for company?"

"No, not today," she said.

She wasn't up to seeing or talking to anyone. She just wanted to be alone, with no expectations. She wanted to insulate herself with warmth, whether it came from her comforter or the sun. She wanted to rest, to sleep. She felt defeated, an emotion she was experiencing more often lately. She thought losing weight, getting thinner, would counter the confusing thoughts and feelings that had been increasing with the continued absence of her father. It was true that she had felt excited, almost elated, watching the numbers on the scale go down. In fact, she had been feeling pretty good this week, until her dad had called. She had come down hard from the high she'd been on.

"She's not feeling too well today, Jeremy. She's resting," Mary Baxter told the handsome young man standing on her front porch, concern on his face.

She remembered the time Jeremy Duscana had stood on that porch, at the tender age of three, his chubby hand held firmly by his mother. "Pretty!" he'd said, pointing to her blond hair. He was a little charmer, even then.

"Oh, okay Mrs. Baxter...um, will you ask her to call me, once she's feeling better?" he asked, his voice full of worry.

"Of course Jeremy, and don't worry, she'll be fine by tomorrow, I'm sure," she said, closing the door.

He stood there a second longer, then headed back to his house. She had seemed to recover well last night, very well, if her goodnight kiss was any indication of how she was feeling. The thought that she was blowing him off, regretting the time she'd spent with him, made him feel physically sick. No, that couldn't be it. She had melted in his arms, had laughed and smiled, and truly seemed to enjoy herself. Still....

Beth's phone beeped, alerting her to a text message. It was from Rachel.

"How ya feelin today???"

"Eh...im k. Tired. How was your night?" Beth wrote back.

"Amazing!"

"OO DETAILS NOW! TELL ME EVERYTHING!"

"Nothing...everything...have to talk face to face..cyaa"

"Later" Beth wrote, and put her phone back on the small table next to her chair. Then she rolled over.

Rachel put her phone on her nightstand and was about to grab her iPod when a knock on the door stopped her. "Come in," she called.

Her mother opened the door. "Hey, didn't hear you come in last night," she croaked.

Rachel looked at her mother, disgusted. She was wearing a pair of super short and tight shorts that were meant for a girl Rachel's age. She topped those with a skin tight hot pink t-shirt that drew attention to her ridiculously large boobs. Her bleached blond hair was tied up in a matching pink scrunchy and a pair of plastic pink hoops dangled from her ears. Surprisingly, she wasn't wearing any make-up. The contrast of her middle-aged face with the adolescent ensemble would have been very comical to Rachel, if it wasn't her mother.

"I didn't know you were waiting up," Rachel said in her most bored tone.

Her mom glanced around the room, then leaned against the door, "I was up!" she said defensively. "I was up 'til six o' clock!"

Rachel's face fell. If her mother had been up partying until six, then she had indeed heard Rachel come in around that time. She glanced up to find a triumphant look on her mother's face.

"Yeah, I heard you...where were you?" she asked in a mean voice.

"I was at a party with my friends," she told her, maintaining eye contact.

Her mother looked away, but only for a moment. "All night?"

"Yeah, what can I say? Like mother, like daughter," she said sarcastically.

Her mother crossed the room, stumbling a bit, and Rachel belatedly realized that she was either still drunk, or drinking already. She scooted back against her headboard, cringing slightly. Her mother stopped short of smacking her, but the anger was seething from her eyes.

"You listen here, little girl. I wasn't always like this, your father drove me to live this way! If you want to stay out all night, doing God knows what, have at it! I don't care!"

Maybe it was the high from her glorious night with Corey, or the way he made her feel about herself, like she was normal. Or maybe she was just tired of hearing the same crap come out of her mother's mouth, but Rachel had enough! Slowly, she got off the bed and stood as tall as she could, facing her mother, who had taken a couple steps back.

"No, you listen to me, Mother Dear," she started in a quiet voice, "my father has been gone for fourteen years. All the decisions you have made since then are yours! Not his. Not mine. You have been a pathetic excuse for a mother! You have no right to judge me, and you will stay the hell out of my life, just as I have stayed out of yours!"

Her mother had backed up through the doorway during Rachel's rant, her eyes as big as saucers. Rachel, who had followed her, felt so good after finally saying the things she had longed to say, she almost smiled at her mother's expression. But she wasn't finished.

"And tell your boyfriends to stay the hell away from me!" Then she slammed the door in her mom's face.

She sat down on her bed with a feeling of triumph, which began to dissipate as quickly as it started. The tears rolled down her cheeks. She laid down and sobbed into her pillow. She let the pain come, let it surface. She sobbed and sobbed, crying for the childhood that never was. She cried so hard she thought it would kill her, but it didn't.

Slowly, the tears stopped and a certain kind of peace replaced the turmoil that had sat in the pit of her soul. She smiled to herself...realizing she had survived the pain she had kept buried for so long, fearful she wouldn't be able to cope with it, scared it would drive her so insane she would never return. But she did return. She was still alive. She was exhausted, but alive.

She glanced at her bathroom door, and took a deep breath. Walking in, she opened the top drawer and pulled out her baggie of razor blades. They had been her little friends, the ones that had gotten her through.

She took off her shirt and looked at the little lines of scars on her left arm. Then she looked at her other arm. She unzipped her shorts and let them drop to the floor. There were scars on both sides of her upper thighs. They were small, but they were definitely there.

Rachel looked at herself in the mirror, finally seeing what she had done. She covered her mouth to keep from screaming. She was rail thin, but not just from the restricting she had started with Beth. She had never been much of an eater, never had an appetite. There hadn't been a lot of weight on her to begin with, so the fact that she hadn't eaten much of anything in almost a week had caused her bones to jut out. She looked at every bone, every scar, then at her face.

"No more," she told herself, "No more!"

She picked up the bag of razors, wrapped it in toilet paper and threw it into the garbage can. A small prickling of fear seeped in, but she firmly pushed it aside.

"I can do this!" she told her reflection.

She had just stood up to her mother, telling her things she'd been dying to say for years. If she was brave enough to tackle that, she was brave enough not to hurt herself anymore.

"Beth!" Mary called to her daughter, who was still asleep outside on the lounger. She watched Beth stir and open her eyes. "Church," she yelled.

Beth gave her a wave and slowly sat up, looking slightly disoriented. "Okay Mom," she yelled back, standing up.

Mary watched her daughter walk towards her and her heart broke. Today Beth walked more like an old woman than a sixteen-year-old girl. Mary knew it was the result of her ex-husband's slow and painful departure from his children's lives....and she hated him for it. His betrayal as a husband paled in comparison to the betrayal he continued to delve out to Beth and Billy, simply by not being there for them. She also knew she was helpless in the matter. As good of a mother as she tried to be, she would never be able to replace their father. Losing him was just something they were going to have to go through and deal with. The thought depressed her completely.

"Do I have to go Mom?" Beth asked when she reached the kitchen.

Mary smiled sadly, "I think today especially, we could all use a little love from God."

Beth sighed, knowing she couldn't argue with a point like that. "Okay, I'll go get ready."

Mary looked at her son, who was playing a game on the computer. "Go shower and get dressed for church."

"'Okay Mom, let me just finish this one last thing then I'll log off," he responded, not taking his eyes off the computer screen.

Mary rolled her eyes, knowing his "one last thing" could range from five more minutes to two more hours. "Five more minutes Billy," she told him, and went upstairs to get ready.

The six o' clock mass was always crowded, mainly because it was the teen mass and had the best music. Most of Beth's friends were there, and even some of Billy's. Mary knew a lot of the parents prior to her divorce, but had grown much closer to them after. They were there for her, bringing her meals at first, then meeting her for a cup of coffee or glass of wine as the months passed. Some of the dads were, or had been, Billy's football coaches, and they continued to exude a bit of a paternal role in his life. Mary was grateful for all of them.

Beth saw Melanie's family, and led her mom and brother to their pew. The girls waved hello, then stood as mass began. She didn't have the heart to sing the songs, her heart was full of anger at her father. She assumed God would understand. During the priest's homily, she tried to listen, tried to apply what he was saying to her own life, but she just couldn't do it. She thought of her father, who used to come to church with them, and wondered what he was doing. Probably out partying with Samantha, she thought to herself. She wondered if he even remembered coming to mass on Sunday night.

Jeremy had an unobstructed view of Beth's pew, and he watched her throughout most of the mass. He was shaken by the look of her. He had never seen her look so exhausted, so defeated. So... depressed. He wished he could have sat with her and held her hand. When mass ended, he approached her. She offered him a weak smile and continued walking with her family.

"You know Sunday's are hard for her lately, don't you Son?" his mother, who was standing beside him, said.

"What do you mean Mom?" he asked, confused.

"Well, you know how her father would pick them up every Sunday and take them somewhere, do something with them?"

Jeremy nodded. He had watched Noel Baxter drive up and honk, not even bothering to get out of the car.

"Have you seen him lately?" she asked.

"No," he said, and closed his eyes.

How could he have been so stupid! Of course, her dad! He had been so wrapped up in his new feelings for her, he hadn't been able to think about much else. Her parent's divorce had been very hard for her, and she had looked forward to those Sundays with all of her heart. Now that Jeremy thought about it, he couldn't remember the last time he saw Mr. Baxter's car in the driveway.

Beth made herself a bowl of granola with soymilk, and headed upstairs. Her mom didn't comment on her choice of cereal for dinner, understanding it had been an emotional day. She curled up in bed, eating her cereal and trying to read a book. Her phone alerted her to a text message. It was from Jeremy.

"R u ok?" he wrote. For the first time since waking up that morning, she smiled.

"Yeah" she wrote back.

"I don't think so"

"What do u mean?"

"Someone let u down."

Beth sighed, "Yeah..I guess"

"I won't" he wrote.

She thought about that. The one man in her life who she had a basic right to depend on, had deserted her. Now Jeremy was asking her to trust him, with her heart. Her mind flashed to memories of all the times she'd shared with him throughout her childhood. They all had one constant theme...he had always been there for her, always taking her side, always defending her...always loving her, she realized.

Across the street, Jeremy sat in his room staring at his phone, waiting for her response, holding his breath.

"I know" she wrote.

And he breathed.

Beth turned her alarm off and shuffled to the bathroom. She stepped on the scale, not really caring what numbers she saw today. Good thing, because she hadn't lost any weight. She hadn't gained any either, which offered some small relief. Her binge must have thrown things off, she mused. Although she'd thought she'd taken care of the extra food by purging.

"Whatever," she told the scale, and turned to examine her reflection. Bad move. Her eyes were puffy from crying the day before, and her complexion was very pale. She started a hot shower, hoping the steam would help with both.

She began to feel a little like herself by the time she finished dressing. Her eyes were still a bit swollen, but her face held more color than before.

"Hey Mom," she said, walking into the kitchen.

Mary looked at her daughter, noted the swollen eyes, and felt the familiar urge to beat the shit out of her ex-husband. Over the last year, she had learned to cope with the fact that he'd destroyed an eighteen year marriage. It had been the hardest year of her life, with many tears. Motherhood had sustained her, and for the first time in a long time, the constant heartache that plagued her had begun to dissipate. However, it was quickly being replaced by an anger so great, she was sure that she could take him down if they were ever pitted against each other.

"Hungry?" she asked with a smile.

"Not really, but I'll force down a grapefruit," Beth answered.

A grapefruit was not what Mary had in mind when she'd suggested breakfast. Her maternal instinct wanted to stuff Beth full of eggs, toast and bacon. It also warned her that, at the moment, Beth was very delicate, so she kept her suggestion to herself. Yet, she couldn't help asking, "Will you at least have a glass of soymilk with it?"

Beth recognized her mother's efforts, and conceded. "Okay."

"Okay, what's wrong?" Jenny asked after Billy got out of the car. She had known something was up with Beth almost immediately after getting in the car.

"Nothing," she said quietly, staring straight ahead at the road.

"Nah-uh. What's goin' on?" Jenny asked in a tone she hoped would make Beth start talking. It didn't.

"Nothing Jen, just drop it, okay?" she asked, glancing her way.

Jenny looked at her friend, observing the dark circles under her eyes and pale skin. Something was definitely going on, she was sure of it. She was also just as sure that Beth wouldn't tell her, yet. Where Jenny spilled all of her deepest, darkest secrets to her friends whether they wanted to hear them or not, Beth stuck to her own timetable on when, where and to whom she would share her innermost thoughts. By the time they were ten, she had learned to read Beth very well and knew when to push her for more info. Everything about Beth was screaming "*Leave me alone!*"

"Alright, fine," Jenny said reluctantly. She saw Mel and Rachel waiting for them in the parking lot, and sighed. Melanie wouldn't practice the same restraint.

"Hey guys!" Melanie greeted as they walked up.

"Hey!" Jenny said enthusiastically. A little too enthusiastically.

"Hey," Beth said quietly, and started walking toward the school.

Melanie's eyebrows drew together, and she ran to catch up.

Rachel gave Jenny a questioning glance, to which Jenny answered, "Don't ask."

Rachel nodded, understanding. Jenny didn't know how Rachel understood without knowing what was going on with Beth, yet she did.

"Hey, what's wrong?" Melanie asked once she reached Beth.

Beth stopped and turned to her three worried friends. She loved them for their concern, but desperately needed them to back off, at least until she could figure out what she was thinking and feeling.

"Listen, I'm fine, really. It's just some stuff going on with my dad, and I don't want to talk about it right now, okay?"

They nodded and hugged her, but it was too much. She knew if she allowed herself to dwell in the comfort of their gesture, she would break down right there in front of school. Abruptly, she pushed away from them, shaking her head. "Please, don't," she whispered, and ran into school.

"Her dad is such a loser," Rachel murmured. "I mean, what a dick, right?" she said more loudly, looking at her friends.

"I still don't get it," Jenny said, "One day, he was there, I mean, really there with them. The next day, he was gone."

"I know," Melanie agreed. "I never understood how Mr. Baxter could just leave them like that, especially for that skank."

"We should key her car or something," Rachel said quietly, still staring at the door Beth had ran through.

"Rachel! That's illegal!" Melanie exclaimed.

"I know Mel, but doesn't abandoning your wife and children deserve something illegal?" she almost yelled at Melanie.

Melanie thought on that a moment, then she nodded. "You're right..you are. But we shouldn't even bother with her. She would have slept with anyone who had money. She's just your typical gold digging Barbie. He's the one who deserves it."

The other two nodded, and they all followed Beth into school.

"I'm not going to play this Goddamn game with you guys. Now, where is she?" Jeremy asked again.

The other girls looked at him. Jenny and Melanie's eyes were as wide as saucers, their mouths partway open. In all the years they'd known him, Jeremy had never spoken to them in that tone. He had never sworn at them either.

Rachel calmly stared back at him and said, "For the second time, we don't know Jeremy."

He took a deep breath, staring at the three girls. He had assumed he would see Beth at lunch, and now that he couldn't find her, his frustration was increasing with every minute. As was his worry.

"Listen, I know you girls are doing some sort of stupid diet. Are you not telling me because of that?"

The girls glanced at each other. Melanie was the first to speak, "First of all, I'm not doing the diet. Secondly, it has nothing to do with the diet, truly."

"I'm not doing the diet anymore," Rachel said, and the other two girls looked at her. "It's a long story."

Melanie smiled, somehow knowing it was a good story.

"Okay, fine, if it's not the diet, what is it?" he asked.

Jenny bit her lip, "We can't tell you Jeremy. We don't completely know ourselves. Hopefully you'll have better luck than we did."

He knew they were telling the truth, but the knowledge didn't help. In fact, it made him more concerned. If Beth wasn't telling her friends what was bothering her, it was something pretty big. As close as she was with her friends, she was still a private person.

Throughout their childhood, there had been secrets she had only shared with him, and they had been the big ones. In fact, he could only remember three: the time she wet the bed, the time she filled a bag full of bulk candy and walked out of the grocery store without paying, and the day her dad left.

Jeremy had found her, sitting on the floor of the garage, next to her fishing pole. He had walked in looking for her, and stopped dead in his tracks. She clutched the pole, sobbing. She looked at him, and he felt his heart rip out of his chest. There was so much pain reflected on her face, he didn't know how she stood it. He sat down next to her and held her while she sobbed.

They had never spoken about it, but he knew she hadn't told the girls. In fact, he had always suspected that she never fully divulged the pain of her dad's abandonment to anyone. Beth was more the type to hold it in and deal with it any way she could.

Suddenly something dawned on him. "Did she say anything about her dad to you guys?" he asked.

The girls slowly nodded.

"Thanks," he said, and left.

The velvet hat kept flopping into her eyes, and she pushed it up for the second time, only to have it flop back down again.

"Fine," Beth told the hat, and hung it back on its hook.

She scanned the other hats hanging on the wall, and chose a black fedora. She turned to the mirror to check her reflection, and almost screamed when she saw Jeremy reflected back at her. She spun around and yelled, "What are you doing, trying to scare me to death?"

He smiled and shook his head. Once he found her, he'd just wanted to watch her for awhile.

"No, of course not," he said, walking over to her. He glanced at the hats, and grabbed a poor boy off a hook. "What do you think?" he asked, putting it on and giving her a model's pose.

She looked at him, trying desperately to stay mad at him for scaring her.

"No?" he asked. He put the poor boy back on its hook and grabbed a jester's hat. "How 'bout now?" he said, making a goofy face at her.

She couldn't help it, she giggled. He had always been able to make her laugh, even in the worst of times.

"How did you know where to find me?" she asked.

Jeremy stared down at her, happy to see her smiling, if only a little. He glanced around the backstage area of their drama department. Beth had auditioned for every school play since they were five.

"Oh, it wasn't that hard," he said, giving her a gentle smile. "You okay?" he asked, more serious.

She looked away, focusing her attention on choosing another hat off the wall. "Yeah, I'm fine."

"The girls seem a little worried about you."

She decided on a hat similar to Robin Hood's, and walked back over to the mirror. "I know, but I'm fine."

Jeremy knew that tone. He knew she wasn't fine, but he knew she wasn't telling either.

"Okay," he relented, and reached into his book bag. She watched him pull out a salad, and sighed. "Ya gotta eat," he said, holding the salad out to her.

Beth didn't know if she wanted to scream at him or throw herself into his arms, or both. On one hand, she was annoyed with him for bringing her food, something she didn't want...or need. On the other, knowing she was on her "diet", he had at least been thoughtful enough to bring her a salad. She felt tears welling up and blinked rapidly.

"Thanks, but I'm not hungry," she said, her voice sounding a bit like a frog's. She cleared her throat.

Jeremy was only willing to let her get away with so much. Not talking was one thing, but not eating was an entirely different matter. He set the salad on a table the drama club used in kitchen scenes, and walked over to her.

With her back up against him, they stared at each other in the mirror. Slowly, he removed the Robin Hood hat, dropping it on the floor. She watched his hand move her hair off her neck, and shivered. Still holding eye contact, he smiled. Then he leaned down and gently kissed her neck, over and over.

He pressed kisses into her skin, searing her with each one. Her muscles began to relax and she leaned against him fully, raising her hand above her, finding the hair at the nape of his neck. He moved up to her ear, touching his tongue to the lobe, and felt her sharp intake of breath. He wrapped his arm around her waist, and worked his way across her cheek, finding her mouth. The moment their mouths touched, she turned into his arms, molding her body to his. Their mouths met, then parted, then met again, over and over. After what seemed an eternity, he slowed them down with gentle kisses on her mouth, nose and eyelids. Then he just held her.

She looked up at him, and there was no way he could mistake what she wanted. "I thought you weren't hungry?" he teased.

"I'm not, for food..." she whispered, smiling.

He looked down at her, fighting his own desire. "That's too bad," he said, sighing, "because I require a beautiful girl to join me for lunch."

"That's not fair," she murmured, leaning up on her tip-toes to kiss him again.

Pulling his head back he said, "Maybe not, but in order to keep my strength up, you know, for kissing, I need to eat. And so do you."

She looked up at him, weighing her chances of getting another kiss without eating her salad, and knew he had won. "Fine, let's eat," she grumbled, moving out of his arms and walking over to the table.

She stared down at the salad he'd made for her. She had to give him credit, it looked really good. He'd included all of her favorites, spinach, broccoli, carrots, purple onion and peas. He also added garbanzo beans, which he knew she couldn't resist.

"What kind of dressing did you use?" she asked him suspiciously.

She felt him walk up beside her, and knew he was staring down at the salad too.

"Balsamic, but not too much, I promise," he said so sincerely, she almost cried.

Instead, she sat down, grabbed the plastic fork he'd brought, and dug in. She glanced up at him, chewing reluctantly, "Happy?" she asked.

Jeremy burst out laughing, and sat down next to her, taking out his sandwich. He also took out two bottles of water.

"Yes," he said, and she believed it. Sitting with him at the pretend kitchen table, she almost felt happy herself, a little.

Later, sitting at her computer, she wasn't feeling that happiness anymore. She was writing an email to her father, asking him about the plans he said he was going to make for Sunday. She was feeling more disgusted than unhappy. Disgusted with herself for writing to him already. She'd hoped to make it to at least Wednesday, but didn't. She missed him so much, she couldn't control herself. She hit the send button and went downstairs to get through dinner.

Nine

The following morning, Beth's spirits were slightly lifted when the scale showed that she'd lost another pound. Her clothes were so loose on her, she decided to wear a baggy shirt, hoping it would hide the fact that her shorts were falling down. Her mother had left for an early meeting, which allowed her to eat her grapefruit and water in peace.

"You're too skinny," her brother mumbled.

"What?" she asked, surprised he'd even spoken to her. He had appeared so engrossed in the television that she'd assumed he hadn't even noticed her entrance.

Billy glanced at her, then back at the tv. "You need to eat more," he said.

"No I don't," she said back to him, defensively.

Billy rolled his eyes and mumbled, "Whatever" as he left the room to get his backpack.

This was not good. If her brother was able to notice how much weight she'd lost, everyone else would too.

"So, I have a confession to make," Jenny said as soon as Billy shut the car door.

Beth glanced at her, "What?"

"Well..I'm not dieting anymore, please don't be mad!" Jenny said, the words rushing out.

For a moment, Beth *was* mad. How could Jenny abandon her? She almost felt... betrayed. She needed a partner, didn't she?

"I can tell you're upset," Jenny continued. "I'm sorry."

Beth barely heard her, she was thinking back over the last week and a half, realizing that she had been able to do this on her own. Having Jenny do it with her had been a great source of support, but she didn't need her in order to lose.

"Hello? Are you going to stop speaking to me?" Jenny asked, her voice laced with anxiety.

Beth shook herself and focused on her friend. Smiling, she said, "No, of course not! It's totally okay, I'm fine doing this on my own. Why are you stopping?"

Relieved, Jenny smiled. "Well, remember Corey's cousin at the party?"

She nodded.

"He's been calling me!"

"That's great!" Beth said, and she meant it. He had seemed like a nice guy, very outgoing. They were perfect for each other.

"I know! So, he wants to take me out this weekend, and I don't want to worry about what to eat and what not to eat, it's just too..."

"Limiting?" Beth offered.

"Yeah!" she exclaimed. "Exactly. I just want to have fun with him, you know?"

Beth nodded again. She knew. She wanted that too, to be carefree again. It seemed that over the last year, she had slowly been losing that part of herself. In its place, a heaviness had taken over her soul.

"It's cool Jen, I'm happy for you! No worries," she told her.

"Thanks," Jenny said, smiling. She looked at her friend, taking her in. It was obvious she had stuck to the "diet". "Um, how much longer are you going to keep dieting?" she asked hesitantly.

"I don't know, until I reach my goal weight, I guess," Beth said matter-of-factly.

"How much further 'til you get there?"

"Three pounds and I'll be 110," she answered.

"Then you'll stop?" Jenny stated more than asked.

"Uh huh," Beth mumbled, turning into a parking space. She turned off the car and got out before Jenny could ask her any more questions, because she knew she couldn't give her honest answers.

"Hey!" Melanie greeted them, her usual jovial self. "Guess who asked me out?"

Beth thought for a moment, then her eyes got wide. "Dylan?"

Melanie nodded so fast Beth thought her head might fall off. "Yes!!! I can't believe it! I've been waiting for that boy to come around for so long, it had become a habit!"

Beth and Jenny laughed and hugged Melanie.

"I'm so happy for you Mel," Jenny said excitedly.

"Yeah, I gotta give you credit girl. He better live up to the wait!" Beth said.

But Melanie shook her head. "He doesn't have to. I've watched him from the sidelines for what feels like my whole life. I've seen his successes and his failures. And I've loved him through it all. He just has to be himself and we'll be fine."

"Wow!" Jenny said, and Melanie laughed.

"You've always been the wise one, you know," Beth said quietly.

And it was true. Melanie had always been their guide, their protector, even their mentor at times. She was an incredibly strong woman at the tender age of sixteen. Dylan didn't know what he was getting himself into.

"Who's she texting so much?" Jenny asked, motioning to Rachel.

Melanie glanced at Rachel, who was completely focused on her phone. "Who do you think?"

"Corey," Beth surmised, and Melanie nodded. "How much are they texting?"

"It's not how much they're texting. It's how much they're texting, talking, seeing each other. I swear that girl's in love. Don't mention it to her though, she'll just deny it," Melanie mumbled.

Rachel sent another text and walked over to her friends. "Ready?" she asked with a big smile.

Beth thought she'd never looked more beautiful.

"Hey, I've been lookin' for ya!"

Rachel shut her locker, turned around, and bit her lip shyly. "Oh yeah, why?" she asked, looking up at Corey. Just the sight of him filled her with excitement. She stared at his mouth, thinking about how his kisses made her feel.

Corey watched her eyes move to his mouth. He leaned down and brushed his lips to hers, pushing her back against the locker. "Can you guess?" he whispered, his lips moving back and forth.

She didn't need to guess. He straightened, and she sighed. How on earth she ended up with a guy like Corey, she'd never know. Yet here he was, kissing her, in view of everyone at school! He was almost proud to be with her. Rachel sure was proud to be with him!

She had discovered that below Corey's easy-going surfer exterior, was a really smart young man, always eager to learn new things. When he initially asked her out, she'd worried they wouldn't click intellectually. The night of his party had diffused any doubts about their compatibility. She'd been surprised to realize he was actually very well read, and they spent most of the night together talking books, and kissing. Around three am, she curled up in his arms and fell sound asleep.

"Was there something else you wanted?" she asked, giving him a seductive smile.

He could think of a few more things he wanted, none of which were appropriate for school. "Actually, yeah. Wanna go surfing with me after school?"

Her face went a little pale. "Uh..I don't know how to surf Corey, I thought you knew that."

His smile widened. "I know, I'm gonna teach ya!"

Her stomach turned over, and her eyes became as big as saucers. "Corey," she began in a shaky voice, "There's something I haven't told you.."

His smile faded and he stood up straighter, bracing himself. "What is it?" he asked, all business.

She looked everywhere but at him. More than anything else, she hated admitting weakness about herself. Her crazy childhood had demanded she rely on her strength just to survive sometimes. She never allowed exposure to her weaknesses, fearful they would be her demise. She took a deep breath and finally looked back up at him.

He was still standing rigid, and his face had become tense. He was looking at her intently, waiting. He was also starting to worry. He watched her fidgeting back and forth, working up the nerve to tell him her secret. A thought flashed across his mind. Maybe she was seeing someone else...

"What is it?" he asked again, surprising himself with his forceful tone.

Rachel found herself fascinated with this new side of Corey, but quickly shook herself back to reality.

"Okay, here it is....I'm scared of the ocean," she said quickly, peeking up to see his reaction.

He let out the breath he'd inadvertently been holding and slumped against a locker. "Is that all?" he asked, smiling.

She smiled back and nodded, obviously relieved by his reaction.

He studied her, realizing it had been difficult for her to make the admission. "Well, we're just gonna have to fix that, aren't we?" he teased.

She shook her head, "No, we aren't. I don't go in, Corey, really."

His brows drew together, "Why not?"

Rachel looked thoughtful for a moment. She had never told anyone why she was scared of the ocean, not even the girls. She glanced at his handsome face, and decided maybe it was time to let the nightmare out. Besides, she'd been doing all sorts of crazy stuff lately, from telling her mother off to spending the night in a boy's arms! Why not share her deepest secret too?

"Let's get our lunch first," she said.

She told the girls she was eating with Corey, and met him in the courtyard. The girls had started eating inside again, so they were alone. He'd bought a veggie and cheese sandwich for her and a slice of pizza for himself.

She dug into her sandwich. It had been months, years maybe, since she'd had a real appetite. She felt like she was tasting food for the first time, and it was delicious! So intent was she on eating, that it took her a minute to realize Corey was staring at her, expectantly. She put her sandwich down, took a sip of water and began:

"Okay, so when I was about four years old, my mom and one of her boyfriends at the time, went to the beach. Being that I was so young, she had to take me with her. Me and a cooler of beer. I guess they passed out on the blanket at some point while I played in the sand. Well, I must have toddled over to the water, because all of a sudden I was swept into the ocean by the waves and the current."

She stopped talking for a minute, allowing her mind to conjure up what memories she had from that day. "I just remember feeling like I was being pulled, further and further away from land. I went under. I remember the rushing sound all around me. My eyes hurt from opening them underwater, and all I could see was dark. A light was shining above me, which I now know was the sun. I remember it kind of floated away from me, going higher and higher. I tried to reach out and grab it, but I couldn't. The next memory I have is of people hovering above me. They were the lifeguards of course. They gave me mouth to mouth."

She finished, and gave a loud sigh. Then she stretched her arms above her head and smiled up at the sky. It had been good to tell someone.

Corey wasn't feeling so light-hearted. In all the years he'd been swimming and surfing the ocean, he never witnessed a near drowning. All surfers knew it was a possibility, one that he and his friends had yet to be faced with. The thought that she'd almost died, that he never would have known her, shook him.

"What did your mom do?" he asked quietly.

Rachel swallowed a bite of her sandwich, and laughed. "Oh, that one's classic. Do you know, with all the screaming and yelling that must have been going on while I was in the water, they never woke up! She was awakened by a policeman nudging her. I think they were still drunk, but she put on a good act, you know, hugging me and stuff. Back then, they didn't make you go to the hospital to get checked out. So we just left. She yelled at me the entire way home, told me I was stupid to go by the water when I couldn't swim, stuff like that....I was four years old!"

She felt tears streaming down her cheeks, and quickly began to wipe at them, a habit she'd acquired at an early age. Corey reached out and gently brushed the tears away. Then he leaned over and kissed them, taking the pain with each tear. "Come to the beach with me," he quietly pleaded. "I promise, you'll be safe with me." Exhausted from her emotions, Rachel nodded.

Beth finished her run on the track, and began walking around, trying to cool down. Her heart was racing too fast, and for a moment she felt like she couldn't catch her breath. She began taking deeper, slower breaths, hoping that would slow her heart rate, but it didn't. She couldn't get enough air into her lungs, and her head was feeling all fuzzy. She turned to grab her water bottle, and everything went black.

Jeremy scanned the track, looking for her. After the last bell, he had gone straight to her locker, expecting to find her there. He waited a few minutes, then went in search of Melanie, who was leaning against her locker, talking to Dylan. She told him Beth was on the track. After putting his books away, he headed towards the track, only to be detained by his baseball coach. He felt like he was chomping at the bit by the time they finished their conversation.

Staring at the empty track, he now wondered how long he'd been talking to his coach. He was just about to leave when he noticed something on the opposite side. He walked towards it, then started running once he realized it was Beth. He skidded to his knees beside her, yelling her name. Terrified, he shook her hard. Frantically he looked around, hoping to find something that would help his cause. He grabbed her water bottle and poured half of it on her face. She came to coughing, as some of the water had gotten into her nose.

"It's okay, it's okay," Jeremy soothed, his hands shaking as he helped her sit up. He felt like he couldn't breathe, and dragged some air into his lungs.

She looked at him, her face pale. "What happened?" she asked weakly.

Relieved to hear her speak, he leaned back on his ankles. It took him a minute to find his voice. "I don't know B, I found you lying on the track."

She could hear the fear in his voice and reached out to him. Instantly, she was wrapped in his strong arms. They sat like that on the track, watching the clouds cover the blue of the sky.

"I think it's gonna rain," she said quietly.

Jeremy nodded, but made no move to release her. He was still processing the emotions running through him. He wanted to hold her forever, keep her safe always. He also wanted to shake her, rail at her over what she was doing to herself. He realized he was at a complete loss on how to deal with her. So he relied on the one thing he was sure of, his love for her. Gently, he helped her stand. He grabbed her bag, and they walked across the track, hand in hand.

Later that night, Beth sat in front of her computer, staring at her inbox. Her father hadn't responded, and she thought she was going to lose her mind. She was exhausted after fainting at the track and had barely gotten through dinner. Her mother had demanded to know what was wrong. She was too tired to argue and had told her mom she wasn't feeling well. At least she hadn't lied again. She felt broken, weighed down, lost. Betrayed.

Just then a message came through from Jeremy. She smiled, thinking of how wonderful he'd been today. He had thrown his bike in the back of her car and driven her home. They didn't speak, he just held her hand, steering with the other. He'd given her a gentle kiss on her forehead, and watched her enter the house. She felt tears well up in her eyes as she realized just how much she loved him.

She opened his message, which simply said: "I love you Beth."

She smiled through her tears. Only Jeremy would know that she didn't want to talk right now, didn't want to hear the noise, yet still needed his love, still needed to hear him tell her that he loved her. She was sure there were many girls who would have been offended hearing those three words for the first time via email, but at this point in her life, it was the only way she could hear them.

She was just as sure that Jeremy would need to hear her say them, not write them.

She walked over to her window and opened the plantation shutter. She looked across the street to Jeremy's bedroom window. He was already there, waiting for her. She pressed her hand against the glass.

Jeremy smiled, and pressed his palm on his window. He didn't know how long they stood like that, but when she pulled her hand away, he had to fight the impulse to run downstairs and out the door, to her.

Slowly, she closed her shutters, and her light went off. Still, he stood there a few moments longer.

Ten

For the rest of the week, Beth stayed more and more to herself. She felt like she didn't know how to talk to people anymore, she'd forgotten their language. She was moving in slow motion, while everyone else seemed sped up, living their lives. The girls were supportive as always, but she knew they were becoming increasingly worried. Thankfully, they had the distraction of the boys in their lives to keep them from completely focusing on her situation, whatever that situation was. She found herself studying even more, reading a lot, and exercising compulsively.

She ate just enough to keep herself going, but the dizziness still came at times. Thankfully, she hadn't passed out again. She stopped weighing herself. The scale had become her master, and she was becoming a slave to its numbers. At some point, she realized her eating habits had less to do with wanting to look good, and more to do with something else...something she couldn't define. And that scared her.

Beth had always been an analyzer, even when she was a little girl. The fact that she couldn't figure out her own motives in her self inflicted borderline starvation did not sit well with her. So with the last ounce of rational thought she had, she put the scale back under the sink and shut the door, firmly.

Jeremy was always there, even when she couldn't see him, she knew he was there. His unconditional support and love touched her deeply, yet she couldn't find the words. It seemed the numbness was beginning to take over completely, and she welcomed it. He'd asked her out on Friday, but she'd declined.

Instead, she found herself sitting in her room staring at her computer screen. Her dad had finally written back. She re-read it for the fourth time:

"Hey Sweetheart, I will pick you guys up Sunday morning, and we'll go out on the boat!

See you then,

Dad"

She leaned back in her chair, trying to sort through her feelings. There was a part of her, a big part, that was literally elated over the fact that he had planned a fun day for them. There was also a part of her that was scared to trust him again, afraid of what would happen if he let her down, again.

She was also so angry. Angry that he had caused her to distrust him. His actions and decisions continued to confuse and frustrate her. He was slowly becoming a stranger, someone she didn't know or understand. At the same moment that she wanted to protect herself by pushing him out of her life, she was just as compelled to reach out and grab him…and hold on for dear life.

He seemed to be slipping further away from her, to a point where she was finding it difficult to recognize the father he had once been. She struggled with the fact that her dad had been her best friend for most of her life, and now seemed to be blowing her off like he would an acquaintance.

Beth's head was spinning and the feeling of panic came back. She remembered it from before. She was paralyzed in the chaos of her mind, wanting to move, to do something, anything, but she couldn't. She just sat there, crying while the pain spread through her veins, through her soul.

Then she heard a sound. It was light, like a branch brushing the house as the wind hits it. She blinked and wiped the tears from her eyes. She jumped when she heard the sound again, louder this time. It came from her window. Opening her shutters, she peered out.

There, standing just below her window, was Jeremy. He was digging through her mother's flowers, searching the mulch for a rock. Beth laughed, thinking of the trouble he would get in if her mother caught him threatening her precious plants. He found what he was looking for as she opened her window, and stopped himself just in time from throwing a rock directly at her.

"What are you doing?" she whispered down to him.

He smiled big. "I brought you something," he said, waving it above his head.

She tried to see what he held in his hand, but it was too dark. "What is it?" she asked.

He glanced around and whispered, "Can you come down?"

Beth sighed. She didn't want to see anyone, especially with puffy eyes from crying. But, as usual, she didn't want to say no to him.

"Okay, I'll be right down."

She closed the window, threw a large t-shirt over her pajama tank and shorts, and quietly went downstairs. Her mom had gone to bed an hour ago, and she assumed Billy had fallen asleep listening to his iPod. She punched in the alarm code, and opened the door. The warm breeze floated over her face as she stepped onto the porch, and for a minute she stood there, breathing in the scents of the Florida night.

Jeremy was waiting in the shadows of the porch, and as he watched her, desire poured through him. She looked around. Seeing him, she walked over to the corner he was standing in. She had almost reached him when he said in a low voice, "I should warn you, if you get much closer, I may have to kiss you."

Beth stopped short. Kissing him had been the last thing on her mind. She knew if she let him kiss her, she would feel, and some of the numbness that was protecting her soul would dissipate. She didn't think it was a risk she was willing to take.

He watched her in her state of indecision. If he stepped forward and reached for her, she would be his. Yet, he made no move. He needed the decision to be her own. She leaned forward, and he started to reach for her. She quickly drew back from him, and he let his hands fall to his sides.

"What did you bring me?" she asked, her voice sounding breathless...sexy.

He took a deep breath, trying to get control of himself, and his body. He held something out to her, which she took.

"It's a CD," he said, stating the obvious.

"Who's it by?" she asked, not able to tell in the darkness.

"The Grateful Dead...I figured you like them, you know..cuz you have that shirt.." he said, remembering the day he saw her washing her car.

She thought for a minute, trying to remember what shirt he was talking about. Then she remembered.

"Oh! That was my cousin Jason's shirt. He left it at the house. I figured it was a good shirt to wash the car in..you know, instead of messing up one of my own," she said, smiling.

"Oh," he said flatly. "Um, well...you know, they're really good. They're different, but amazing at what they do. You should check 'em out."

She was so touched that he had brought her something to lift her spirits, in the middle of the night no less, that she would have listened to it even if it was Oscar the Grouch singing.

"I will," she told him. Then she leaned up on her tiptoes and kissed his cheek. "Thank you Jeremy," she whispered into his ear.

Jeremy couldn't help himself, he shivered. He clenched his hands to keep from grabbing her, and stood frozen as she began to move away. Then she made her mistake, she hesitated right near his mouth. He put his hand on her waist, holding her there. He kissed her, slowly, his tongue moving deeper and deeper into her mouth. Her body fit against his, and he reached down, grasping her bottom. She moaned, and Jeremy thought he would die.

He turned and pushed her up against the wall of the house. Their kiss turned into something that was quickly getting out of control. He moved from her mouth to her ear, then her neck. His hands moved up her body, under her large t-shirt, making contact with her tiny tank top. He pushed up under her tank, and froze.

Lifting his head, he began examining her body with his hands. Somewhere in her passion drugged mind, Beth began to realize that he was touching her differently now, almost...clinically.

"What's wrong?" she whispered, barely able to get the words out.

Slowly he felt her sunken belly, then moved up over her protruding ribs. He moved to her back and felt her back ribs. They weren't as prominent as her front, but they were there. Gently, he pulled her tank top back down, withdrew his hands, and straightened.

"Beth," he started, and had to clear his throat. "How much weight have you lost?"

He might as well have thrown a bucket of ice water on her. She swallowed. "What?"

Jeremy sighed. "You've got to stop, you know that, right? You're losing too much."

She stared into his dark face, feeling ugly and ashamed. "Thank you for the CD," she said through tears, pushing past him, heading toward the door.

"Beth, wait!" he said, trying to grab her.

She was too quick though. It shut in his face.

Eleven

"What are you getting ready for?"

Rachel paused from making herself a sandwich, and turned toward her mother. "I'm going to the beach today."

Her mother burst into hysterics, pointing her well manicured finger at Rachel. "You? Goin to the beach? Yeah right!"

Rachel took a deep breath, biting her lip. She was already struggling to keep her emotions in check, and a fight with her mother wouldn't help any. "I go to the beach with my friends sometimes."

Her mother looked her up and down, and said, "Yeah, but you have a bathing suit on. You never wore a suit before to the beach!"

"Yeah, well today I am. Is that okay with you?" she said sarcastically.

Her mother straightened. "Fine with me! I'm having a friend over tonight, so the later the better, if you know what I mean."

Rachel stared at her mom. "Yes, unfortunately, I know what you mean," she said, and turned back around to finish packing her lunch.

She heard her mom shuffle away, and relaxed a little, happy to have escaped the predictable fight. Corey sent her a text that he was going to be there in two minutes, so she quickly shoved her lunch in a bag, as well as her towel and sunscreen. She ran out the door and saw his old Volkswagen bus coming down the road.

He stopped in front of her house, yelling to her from the open window, "Ready?"

She stood on her front lawn, staring at the surfboard tied to the top of the bus. Was she ready? She wasn't so sure...

Corey watched her making up her mind, and gently said, "Come with me Rachel, let's go have some fun."

She smiled, took a deep breath, and got in the bus.

They had been driving a few minutes when he asked, "Hey Rach, you listen to Blues Traveler?"

"A little, why?"

"Do you know their song, 'Just Wait'?"

She thought for a moment, then shook her head. "Is it good?"

He looked at her, and smiled. "Yeah, it's good. It reminds me of you."

Rachel smiled shyly. A boy had never, ever told her that a song made him think of her. She made a mental note to download the song as soon as she got home.

Her happiness was short lived. As soon as they pulled into the parking lot, her stomach became full of butterflies. "Corey.." she said, reaching for his hand.

Instantly he took it. "It will be okay," he said, giving her hand a reassuring squeeze.

She nodded and got out of the bus. She grabbed their bags while he untied the surfboard. The ocean breeze caused her hair to fly in a million different directions, and she stopped to tie it back.

She stood there a moment, looking at the ocean. Where most people saw beauty, she saw death.

"Rachel!" Corey hollered to her. She gave herself a mental shake and followed him down the beach.

"Good waves today!" he told her excitedly.

She looked out at the waves, and thought she was going to puke.

"Ready?" he asked, turning to her.

"What? Now? Already?" she exclaimed. "No!"

He just laughed, stripping off his shirt, and Rachel's mouth went dry. He had an amazing body, and in a way, she was seeing it for the first time. Her eyes took him in from head to toe, and back up again.

Corey was no longer smiling, he was looking at her very intensely, in a way that made her feel beautiful. Slowly, she pulled off the oversized tunic that she used as a cover up, revealing her bikini clad body underneath. For the rest of her life, she would never forget this moment. It was the first time she felt truly gorgeous and seductive. He stood there looking at her, every inch of her. She felt so good she didn't even care about her scars. He didn't seem to notice anyway.

"Um, Corey?" she finally said after he continued to just stand there, staring at her.

His eyes snapped up to hers, and he gave her his crooked smile. "Sorry Rach, you're just so...." He held his hands out to her helplessly, and shrugged his shoulders.

Instinctively, she knew he was at a loss. Feeling more like a woman than a girl, she walked over to him, and gently pushed the hair off his forehead. She leaned up and kissed him softly, pulling away just as he was about to wrap his arms around her.

"Let's go," she whispered.

Corey didn't know if she was talking about surfing, or more kissing, and at the moment he wasn't sure which one he wanted more. It was then that he knew he'd fallen in love with her. He looked at her a moment longer. Then he gave her a hard kiss, grabbed the board and said, "Let's go!"

She closed her eyes and pulled on every bit of strength and confidence she possessed, then turned to face the ocean. She followed him toward the water, and almost jumped when her feet touched the hard wet sand. She dug a toe into it and smiled at the squishy feel.

Corey patiently waited for her, enjoying himself completely.

She took a few more steps to where the waves lapped up onto the sand.

"Deep breaths," she told herself, and stepped into the water. It wasn't cold like she expected. It was perfect, like a bath. She looked up at him, happily surprised.

Corey laughed, because he knew if he didn't he would weep.

"Come on," he said gently, holding his hand out to her.

She took it and let him guide her in, trusting him completely. She was halfway in when a memory from that horrible day assailed her. Once again, she was struggling for air, reaching for the light. Her breathing became shallow, and she looked around frantically, feeling trapped. A cold sweat broke out on her brow and her hands were shaking.

"Hey..Rach.." a voice said gently. But it was muffled by the water.

"Rachel!" the voice shouted, and she found herself leaning against something hard. She rested her head against it, and felt it tighten around her.

"It's okay, everything is okay," she heard Corey say. All at once the sounds of the ocean came back to her and she realized the thing she was leaning against was his chest. He was gently rubbing her back, whispering soothing words. They stood like that until her breathing returned to normal and she stopped shaking.

"You okay?" he quietly asked.

"I think so. I'm sorry," she said, embarrassed.

He leaned his head back, peering down at her. "Sorry for what? Being brave?"

And that is when she cried, because she knew she loved him. And she had to trust him.

"Come on, get on the board," he gently told her, so she did.

He proceeded to show her how to paddle out, swimming alongside her, never leaving her. They didn't go out too far, just enough where she could catch a small wave and he could still stand. He told her what to do when the wave came, to start on her knees, then step up one leg at a time.

Rachel realized that all those times she had sat on the beach while her friends swam had afforded her the luxury of watching the surfers, including him. She knew the moves of a surfer by heart.

They waited, watching for the right wave.

All of a sudden he said, "Okay, ready, Go!" and gave the board a push.

Always a quick study, she got up, and screamed as she rode the wave. She screamed, letting go of the fear, the anxiety, the memories. It was immediately replaced by pure joy.

When she reached the shore, she jumped off the board and turned toward Corey, jumping up and down.

"I did it! I did it!" she yelled to him over and over. She got back on the board and paddled herself right back to him. "I did it Corey!" she yelled again.

He nodded, a huge smile on his face.

As she got closer, she intended to compliment him on his teaching skills, but her breath caught once she reached him.

His eyes were shining brightly with unshed tears. "You did it! You're amazing Rachel," he said, holding onto the board.

She slid off, right into his arms, kissing him with every ounce of love inside of her.

"She did it," Beth said softly.

"She sure did," Melanie agreed.

"I can't believe it!" Jenny said, as tears raced down her cheeks.

They were standing under the gazebo that overlooked the beach, leaning against the rail. Corey had been thoughtful enough to let them know about Rachel's big moment. Good thing, because she hadn't told them.

"Does anyone have any tissues?" Beth asked.

Melanie reached into her bag, and passed tissues to her two best friends. Then she grabbed some for herself. "It's truly amazing, it really is," she said, dabbing her eyes.

They had watched the entire event unfold. When Rachel had stepped in the water, Beth had grabbed Melanie and Jenny's hands. Together, the three of them held their breaths, watching, waiting. When she caught her wave, the girls first laughed, then cried, in celebration of their friend's accomplishment. They had never seen Rachel so happy, so full of life.

"I think she loves him," Beth said quietly.

"Wonder if she's told him yet?" Jenny asked.

"I'm just so happy for her," Melanie said, and the other two nodded. She turned her attention to Beth. "So, what about you?"

Startled, Beth looked at her. "What about me?"

Melanie cocked her head to the side, looking at Beth sadly. "You know what I mean."

"No I don't, I'm fine," she said, turning her attention back to the ocean. Melanie glanced at Jenny.

"Beth," Jenny began, "You know we love you, and we're worried. You aren't around as much anymore, and you have lost too much weight."

Beth pushed away from the railing and started walking to her bike. Her friends followed.

"Beth..." Melanie said.

Suddenly she turned around and yelled, "What? I'm fine!" She got on her bike and headed for home.

"We have to give her space," Jenny murmured.

"We have been giving her space Jen! Too much space maybe," Melanie replied.

They walked back over to the railing, and watched Rachel catch another wave. "I think she's finally dealing with it," Jenny said quietly.

Melanie nodded, "I had assumed the same thing. You know she was acting too "okay" after he left. She wouldn't talk about it, nothing."

"I know. It got to the point where I was scared to bring it up, cuz I didn't want to upset her."

"Well, it's good she's dealing with it, but the way she's dealing with it is...destructive."

"Should we talk to Jeremy?" Jenny asked, glancing at Melanie.

Beth would not be happy if they went to Jeremy. The girls always had a love/hate relationship with him, mainly due to competition for Beth's attention. The subject of Jeremy had caused many arguments among them when they were younger. Yet, over the last couple years, they had formed a kind of truce with him.

Melanie thought on this, and nodded. "We have to, it's her safety we're talking about now."

Just then, Rachel caught site of her friends. Melanie and Jenny had to control the urge to duck out of sight. Instead, they waved and gave very excited thumbs up.

Rachel stared up at them and mouthed the words, "Thank you".

Mary picked up the marigold plant and placed it in the hole she had dug. Gently, she placed soil around the new addition to her front yard landscape, and firmly pushed it down. She leaned back on her ankles and wiped her brow, examining the new row of plants. Hearing a noise, she glanced over her shoulder to see Beth riding up the driveway on her bike.

"How was it?" she asked her daughter.

Beth got off her bike and leaned it against the garage door. "It was good..she did it!" she told her mother. "She was amazing."

Mary smiled. "Good, I'm glad. I'm sure she was happy to have you there supporting her."

She walked over to where her mother was working. "She didn't know I was there. I mean, I left before she saw me."

Mary looked up, shielding her eyes from the sun. "Well, why did you do that?"

Beth looked away and said, "I don't know, just wanted to get home I guess."

Mary nodded, and started digging another hole. "Are you looking forward to tomorrow, with your dad?"

She watched her mom's hands move in the dirt. "Yeah, sure...I don't know. I'm kind of nervous. Isn't that weird?"

Mary thought for a moment, then shook her head. "No, I don't think so. It's hard to face something you aren't sure of, isn't it?"

She met her mother's eyes, and for the briefest moment, she understood herself. "I'm gonna take a shower," she muttered, and went inside the house.

Mary watched her daughter go in. She grabbed another marigold plant and got back to work.

Beth undressed for her shower and stared at the scale. She took a deep breath and stepped on. 108 pounds reflected back. She was two pounds below her goal weight. The feeling of euphoria she expected never materialized. She examined herself in the mirror.

When she started her "diet", she thought her body would resemble a more "Christine McCady" body. Yet, she saw few changes. Her ribs were showing more, as well as her collarbone, but they didn't really qualify as major changes. They were inevitable changes as a result of weight loss. What she wanted to see wasn't there.

The fact that she couldn't define what she was looking for didn't matter, she just knew it wasn't there. She turned around, looking at her back where her ribs were starting to show, and idly wondered if her father would notice her weight loss. Disgusted with herself, she turned on the shower.

"Hi Mrs. Baxter," Jeremy said, walking up the driveway.

"Hi Jeremy! How are you today?" Mary asked, wiping her forehead.

"I'm good. Your flowers look great as always!" he said, taking in the multitude of color.

She followed his gaze. "Yes, well...I enjoy it..." she said, her voice trailing off.

He looked at her, and cleared his throat. "Um, is Beth home?" he asked.

Mary smiled, "Yes, she's inside."

"Thanks," he said, and headed toward the door.

"Jeremy?" she asked.

He turned. "Yes Mrs. Baxter."

She stood up, and walked over, gesturing for him to sit in one of the white wooden rocking chairs on the front porch. She sat in the matching one beside it.

"Jeremy," she began, "I have to ask you something...."

"Yes?" he asked, watching her. She seemed nervous, and very unsure.

"It's about Beth..."

"What about her?"

Mary hesitated, biting her lip. She looked him right in the eye and asked, "Do you know what is going on with her?"

He had expected as much. He knew Mrs. Baxter was worried about Beth. Anyone with half a brain would see how much weight she had lost in such a short period of time. The fact that she was also withdrawing from everyone around her had begun to disturb him so much, he was finding it difficult to concentrate on much else. Rachel,

Melanie and Jenny had shown up at his house about an hour before, full of worry and love for their friend. He had been mildly surprised the girls had come to him, but glad they did. It now seemed that her mother was turning to him as well.

"Do you mean about her weight?" he asked.

She nodded.

"I'm not sure why she's determined to lose so much weight," he began, then hesitated, glancing at Mary. "Mrs. Baxter, I'm sure you know that it's been hard for her this past year…"

She looked away and sighed. "I know..I know. It's been..horrible," she finished, giving Jeremy a sad smile. "I've tried to keep things the same for them. The same family traditions, same rules, same restaurants. It seemed so much had changed when their father left, they needed that consistency."

He thought on that a moment, cocking his head to one side, his brows drawn together. "It sounds like you've been trying to hide the change by covering it up with the same."

Mary looked at him, wondering how a seventeen-year-old boy could be so wise. She thought about all of the times over the last year when she had just quickly kept going. Afraid that if she slowed down, Beth and Billy would have too much time to sit and dwell on what their father had done. She had been so hell-bent on nothing changing, not realizing that it already had. She had figuratively covered their house in sheets, covered it all up, thinking her kids wouldn't see.

Yet she was the one who had been blinded, not them. They were too brave to try to hide behind old traditions, behind over-bright smiles...behind an award winning garden. They had been trying to face their father's desertion head-on, while she had been more focused on making sure Saturday was still pizza night. She closed her eyes and took a deep breath.

"Are you okay Mrs. Baxter?" he asked, worry showing in his eyes.

Mary opened her eyes, and for the first time since her husband had left her, she knew what to do. She stood up, and Jeremy stood with her. She clasped both his hands, looking up at him.

"Thank you Jeremy. You've always been such a good boy, and you have turned into a wonderful young man."

"Ummm...thank you," he said, feeling utterly embarrassed.

Seeing his discomfiture, she smiled and patted his hand. "I'll get Beth for you!"

He was so lost in thought he didn't hear when Beth came out. She stood there, watching him slowly rocking in the chair, while a memory of another time Jeremy had sat in that same chair came back to her. It had been the day after he'd broken the head off her favorite Barbie doll. She had been so mad at him, she told him to go home and that she never wanted to play with him again.

The next day, she was playing in her room when her mother told her that he was outside, wanting to see her. She stood to her full eight year old height and haughtily told her mom that she never wanted to speak to him again! Her mother had given her a look and told her to march her little bottom downstairs.

She'd come out of the house, full of attitude and ready to kick him off her property. But as she stepped on the porch, she found Jeremy nervously rocking, holding a package in his hand. Seeing her, he'd jumped off the rocker so quickly, it nearly toppled over.

"Hi Beth," he said, looking up at her.

Even though he was a year older than her, she'd been two inches taller. She crossed her arms and peered at him expectantly.

He held up the package he'd been holding. It was a brand new Barbie doll, just like the one he'd broken. "I took my allowance and bought this for you....I'm sorry I broke your other one."

Beth looked at the package, noticing that the one he bought was wearing a purple polka dot skirt, not a red skirt like her old one. Purple was her favorite color. She reached out and took the package, examining it. Then she looked back at him and said, "I forgive you."

He sighed with relief. "You wanna play?" he asked with a lopsided grin.

She thought a moment longer, then smiled. "Yeah, come on, I just got some new Play-Doh!"

"Cool!" he exclaimed, and they spent the rest of the afternoon destroying her mother's kitchen with their Play-Doh creations.

Jeremy sensed someone was watching him, and turned his head to find Beth staring at him, a half smile on her face. "Hey!" he said, standing up.

The smile faded as she came back to reality. "Hey."

"Are you doing anything right now?" he asked.

She was tempted to make something up, but as usual she couldn't lie to him. "No, just hangin'."

"Cool, let's go for a ride then."

She shook her head. Being alone with Jeremy was the last place she wanted to be. "No, I'm not up for a ride...sorry."

He just smiled. "Get your hoodie, it's windy," he told her.

She looked at him, frustrated because he'd ignored her response. She tried again. "I'm not up for the beach either."

"Are you going to grab your sweatshirt, or should I?"

She wanted to stamp her foot at his arrogance.

"Fine, I'll be right back," she muttered, slamming the door behind her.

"I told you it was windy," Jeremy said, laughing.

Blinded by the hair blowing into her face, Beth quickly tied it back. She glared at him.

"Come on," he said, offering her his hand. Reluctantly she took it, and they walked down to their favorite spot. He spread a blanket out and laid back on it, patting the spot next to him. "Sit."

She took a deep breath, and sat as far from him as possible. He just laughed and scooted closer to her.

"Why did you bring me here?" she asked, staring at the waves breaking on the shore.

He followed her gaze. "It's been too long since you've been here."

"I know."

"Why?" he asked.

"I don't know."

He glanced at her. She looked like she was being swallowed up by her sweatshirt. He didn't even want to contemplate how much weight she'd lost, he just knew it had to stop. She had to stop. He took a deep breath, feeling like he was about to enter a war zone.

"B, you're one of the smartest girls I know, if not the smartest. You must realize how worried everyone is about you."

She nodded slightly and said, "I know."

"Do you know why you're doing this to yourself?" he asked.

She continued to stare at the waves, watching them come in, then go back out again. She wished they could take her with them. She looked at him, her brown eyes filled with confusion, and sadness. "I don't know."

He wanted to take her into his arms. It took all of his will power not to reach out to her, because he knew if he did, she may stop talking. "Is it because you think it makes you...prettier?" he asked.

She thought for a moment. "I used to...I mean, yeah, I thought it would make me look better, I guess. I wanted to look different...be different."

For the life of him, Jeremy couldn't understand why the hell she would want to be anyone other than herself. He stopped himself from saying as much. "Have you reached the weight you were going for?"

"I did, but..it wasn't enough. Once I got there, I was less unhappy about my weight, but I wasn't any happier. Does that make sense?"

"Yeah, sort of.."

"I know it sounds crazy, I do. I feel caught, like I can't get out of something I started. I guess I wasn't prepared. The more weight I drop, the more depressed I feel. I thought it would be the opposite."

"Are you sure it's about weight?"

She looked at him. "What do you mean?"

Jeremy knew this was the moment. This was the reason he had brought her here. She would either shut down completely, or save herself. "B, do you think this might have to do with your dad leaving?"

Her brows drew together. "No, he left a year ago. I started this diet a couple weeks ago."

"Yeah, I know, but...do you think you're just now dealing with him leaving?"

She looked away, but not before he saw the tears. He pulled her into his arms. "It's okay you know," he said quietly, comforting her.

Comfort was the last thing Beth wanted, and she jerked out of his arms. "It's not okay!" she yelled at him. "It's not okay! None of it...none of this is okay!"

He watched her, not sure what she was going to do next. She stood and walked down to the water. After a couple minutes, he followed her. "He left us. How could he leave us Jeremy?" she asked, looking like a wounded child. "We were a family! He was our father. We did everything together!"

"I know," he said.

"It feels like a part of my soul has been ripped out and I don't know how to fill it. I feel like everything in my life is falling apart! Nothing is the way it was, yet my mother insists that we go through the motions of our old life. How can I pretend to live a life that doesn't exist, yet I have no idea how to live this new life that has been thrown at me? I feel dead."

The tears were flowing freely down her face, and she impatiently wiped them away. "I didn't ask for this, I don't want it! My life was great before..it was freakin' perfect! I was daddy's little girl, I felt loved, cherished. Now I feel betrayed, and discarded. He's traded us in for a new one. How could he do that?" she asked, looking at him. "How could he leave us? Doesn't he love us anymore?"

She started sobbing then, and that is when she let him hold her. They stood like that for what felt like hours, while she cried her heart out. Jeremy was at a loss, so he stroked her back. Finally her tears subsided, and he led her back to the blanket.

"Here," he said, grabbing a bottle of water out of his backpack. Then he handed her a sandwich. She looked at it, then at him. "It's your favorite, veggie and cheese," he said, holding his breath, waiting for her to take it from him.

She looked at it again, and slowly reached out, taking it. "Thank you," she said, and for the first time in weeks she was actually hungry.

"Anytime."

It was much later when they returned home, and it was starting to get dark. He walked her up to the door, and leaned down to gently kiss her. She kissed him back so thoroughly that he had to catch his breath when they parted. She smiled, and turned to go in.

Then she turned back around and called to him, "By the way, I like the CD..a lot."

"I knew you would. They are unique, original...like you," he said.

Beth looked at him, standing in the middle of the yard, his thick hair wind blown around his face. "I love you Jeremy," she said quietly, and went inside.

He stood there, frozen. Then he smiled.

"Beth? Is that you honey?" Mary called from the kitchen.

"Yeah Mom," she said. "What are you making?" she asked, entering the room.

"Pesto," her mom said with a twinkle in her eye.

"Pesto? Since when do you make pesto?"

Mary noticed her daughter's red and swollen eyes. Beneath that, she recognized signs of the old

Beth. There was a sense of peace about her and Mary was so happy she thought she might cry. She turned back to the food processor that was chopping up fresh basil from her garden and said, "Since now. Since today! Don't you like pesto?"

"I do, very much. You've just always made red sauce."

Mary looked back at her. "I know. I felt it was time to try something different. What do you think? Are you up to trying something new?"

Beth looked at her mother, who was holding out a spoon filled with pesto for her to taste. She gave her mom a big smile, leaned over and tasted the sauce. It was the best thing she had ever tasted. "New is good," she said.

Mary nodded. "New is good."

It was the first Saturday night in Beth's life when she wasn't surrounded by pizza boxes, but instead, a big bowl of pasta with her mother's instantly famous pesto. She watched Billy slurp up his pasta with all the noise and gusto only a ten year old boy could create, and laughed. Truly laughed. New was good for all of them.

Twelve

"He's here."

Beth turned to look at her mom, standing in her bedroom doorway. "Okay, thanks," she said, and grabbed her bag off the bed.

"Beth! Come on!!" she heard Billy yell from the bottom of the stairs.

She felt a few momentary butterflies in her stomach, so she took a deep breath and quickly went downstairs, her mother following close behind.

"Call me if you need anything, promise?" Mary asked with a worried frown.

She gave her mom a reassuring hug, "It'll be fine, don't worry."

Then she followed her brother, who was carrying their fishing poles, out the door. Her dad was sitting in his silver Mercedes convertible, waiting for them. He gave a wave to Mary, and they were on the road.

"I just have to make a call," he said, getting on his cell phone.

Beth and Billy looked at each other. They hadn't talked to their father since the phone call a week ago, and even then they didn't really talk. As she watched the lush landscaping of the local businesses fly by her window, she realized she hadn't had a real conversation with her father in over a year. When he'd first left, all of their conversations had involved his attempt at explaining why he'd left. His explanations had been weak and random, and had left her more confused than ever.

He built his new life with Samantha, letting his old life fall apart, crumbling around his kids. As each week passed, he spoke to them directly less and less, and now, avoided talking to them altogether...about anything with any meaning at least.

They pulled into the marina and got out of the car. The familiar smells of days out on the boat hit her, and tears unexpectedly formed in her eyes. Quickly, she wiped them away before anyone could see. They had only been to the marina once since her dad left, and that was to meet him for dinner at the restaurant. They hadn't been on the boat with him in over a year, the last time being when they were together, as a family.

She was still feeling a little off balance as they walked toward the boat, and that was before she saw Samantha step onto the dock and wave to them. Beth stopped dead in her tracks. Billy, too focused staring at the Jacks in the water to notice Samantha, realized she had stopped. So he stopped too.

"What's wrong?" he asked. When his sister didn't immediately answer, he followed her gaze, and his face fell. "Shit," he muttered.

Their dad turned around and looked at them. "C'mon guys! Better hurry up, it's getting late!"

Beth looked at Billy. He looked completely stricken, so she couldn't even begin to imagine what her reaction must look like. Their dad either hadn't noticed, or was ignoring it. She wanted to run, to turn away and race as fast as she could. Away from Samantha and her bikini clad body. Away from her father, or this new man inhabiting her father's body. Away from the memories, years and years of memories on their boat, with their mother. Yet she knew she couldn't leave Billy alone in this nightmare.

She stepped forward and put her arm around his shoulders. "Come on, it'll be fine," she said, repeating the exact words she'd told her mother earlier.

Together they walked, trying to draw strength from each other so they would be able to actually step foot on the boat.

"Hey guys!" Samantha yelled to them as they got closer. "Isn't it a beautiful day?"

"Yeah," they muttered, stepping down into the boat.

Beth could tell Samantha was a little put off by their lack of excitement, but she didn't care. Seeing Samantha, with her giant boobs spilling out of her bikini top, work in the galley of their boat made her want to throw up.

Billy helped their dad untie the ropes, and they were off.

They fished. Well, she and Billy fished. Samantha laid out in the sun, her oil covered body glistening. Beth secretly hoped she would get skin cancer, on her boobs. Their dad spent most of his time either up top driving the boat or putting more oil on Samantha. He would check on them once in awhile, but his heart wasn't in it.

For three hours the two of them fished, sitting side by side, as their reality sunk in. It was all gone for them. The days when their dad sat with them, fishing and telling stories, or inappropriate jokes that made them all laugh, were gone. They had grown up on that boat, exploring new snorkeling spots, fishing spots and marinas. They had traveled numerous times down to the Keys for Thanksgiving and summer break. Their mother had made many amazing culinary creations in the small galley, which they'd enjoyed under the stars. That boat had become their second home. Now it felt like a prison.

Samantha's giggling had been their background music for most of the trip. Every time she laughed at something their father did or said, Beth wanted to jump out of her skin and strangle her.

"I hate him," Billy said quietly, staring at the water.

She sighed, "No, you don't."

He turned to her, tears streaming down his face. "I do, I hate him."

She looked at him sadly, and he wiped his arm across his face. "You don't hate him, you hate them," she said, gesturing to the front of the boat, where Samantha and their dad were lying side by side in the sun.

But Billy shook his head. "I don't hate her."

She looked surprised and asked, "You don't?" Then muttered, "I do."

He looked back at the ocean below them. "She's not worth my hate. She's nothing. There are a million of her, there's only one of him. He took him away from us, she didn't."

Beth stared at her brother, while a terrible, crushing pain took control of her heart. He was right, her father had made the decision, all on his own. For months after he'd left, she had focused all of her resentment, all of her pain, on Samantha's pretty little head. But if it hadn't been Samantha, it would have been someone else. As much as Beth had wanted, desperately, to believe that her father had left them for another woman, it just wasn't true. The truth was that their father had left them. Period.

For the rest of her life, Beth was sure she would never understand how or why her dad had made such a decision. A decision that destroyed the lives of the people he was supposed to love and protect.

"Hey! You guys ready to head in and grab a bite to eat?" he yelled from his spot by Samantha.

They looked at each other, and muttered in unison, "Sure."

If the boat had been torture, dinner was a disaster. Her dad spent most of the evening walking around and talking to fellow boaters he'd known for years, or snuggling with Samantha as they sat side by side across the table from them. He whispered something into Samantha's ear, and she glanced at Beth. Warily, she watched Samantha turn her full attention onto her.

"I'm going to the gift shop to take a peek, wanna come?"

Beth glanced at Billy. As usual, he was totally engrossed in eating his dinner, especially because it was filet mignon. He had been sighing between each bite throughout their meal. She was almost jealous of him because he had something to distract himself from the travesty of the day.

She did have to give herself some credit. Even though her stomach wanted to reject it, she forced down half of her dinner. It was the largest amount of food she'd eaten in a long time...and kept down anyway.

"Sure," she said, and followed Samantha to the little gift shop connected to the restaurant. She looked at all the touristy items, not really seeing them. She ran her hands over sweatshirts and bathing suits, not really feeling them. She watched Samantha shop, something she did very well.

"Beth, you should get something for your mother," Samantha said over her shoulder.

"What?" Beth asked, sure that she heard wrong.

Samantha turned to her, "You should get something nice for your mom, you know, because she couldn't come."

Beth stared into Samantha's bright, shining face, while something inside of her built. It rolled up until she felt like she was going to explode. It came out in a burst of laughter. A fit of giggles so hard, she doubled over with it. Samantha, who had started laughing when Beth did, suddenly caught on that the way Beth was laughing wasn't normal. She stared at her as if she was some unknown creature.

She glanced at the cashier, who was also staring at Beth, and whispered, "She's had a bit of a tough time lately."

Hearing this, Beth succumbed to another fit of hysteria.

Now Samantha was starting to get embarrassed. "Beth," she began sternly, "I'm not sure what is so funny, but you are making a scene!"

Beth covered her mouth and stared at Samantha, little giggles escaping through her fingers. Tears of mirth were rolling down her face. She got herself together enough to say, "You're right Samantha! I'll be in the bathroom."

And with that, she high-tailed it out of the store and headed to the restroom, giggling all the way.

While she was dabbing her eyes with a paper towel, she heard a horrible, yet familiar, retching sound coming from one of the stalls. The toilet flushed, and out walked Christine McCady. Beth watched in shock as Christine dabbed the mascara from under her eyes, and rinsed her mouth with water.

She glanced at Beth, who was still staring. "Hey, you go to my school, right?"

Beth nodded, then asked, "Are you okay?"

Christine looked at her questioningly, then gestured to the stall she'd just exited. "Oh that..yeah, of course. Did you just finish?"

In a matter of moments Beth realized Christine had been purging. Mascara was running down her face, and she was blowing her nose. Close-up, Christine had dark smudges under her eyes, and her hair wasn't quite as glowing as Beth remembered. She was rail thin, almost sickly looking.

"You need a breath mint?" she asked, pulling out a Costco sized container of mints.

"Um, sure," Beth replied, blindly putting her hand out.

Christine finished shaking out her hair. "Well, have a good night."

"You too," she said, watching Christine leave the bathroom.

She paused at the door. "By the way, love what you've done with yourself. Ten more pounds and you'll be super hot!"

And she was gone.

Beth looked at herself in the mirror, and for the first time, saw the dark smudges under her eyes. Her hair hung loose, laying flat against her head. Her skin was very pale. Hesitantly, she lifted her oversized t-shirt, exposing her stomach. All of her ribs showed, and her stomach was sunken in. For the first time, she saw how frail her arms looked.

She also finally saw how she'd chosen to deal with her father's abandonment...by destroying herself.

She returned to the table, lost in thought.

"Oh, look! The guy who sings is here!" Samantha exclaimed, clapping her hands. "He's sooo good!" she told Beth, as if they were the best of friends.

"Hm," Beth said.

The man had an acoustic guitar with him, which he played beautifully.

"This is stupid!" Billy mumbled.

Just then he started into an old REO Speedwagon tune, and Billy gave her a you've-got-to-be-kidding-me! look. She bit her lip to stop herself from smiling. Then the words from the song, "It's Time for Me to Fly" hit her. She listened to the lyrics and glanced at her dad, who was now dancing with Samantha next to their table.

She thought about all of the times he'd danced with her, at weddings, at parties, in their living room on pizza night. He always said, "I love dancing with my little girl." Then just like that, he found a new partner.

"C'mon," she said to Billy. "We're outta here."

"Yesss!" he said, following her out of the restaurant, the song leading the way. While they walked back to the boat to grab their stuff, she called their mom.

Then she stood on the boat one last time. She closed her eyes, allowing herself to relive the memories.

"We aren't gonna be on this boat again, are we?" Billy asked beside her.

She opened her eyes and shook her head. "I don't think so B. Dad...he's onto another life, you know?"

He nodded, "I know."

Then he went down to the galley, and came back with a sign. It was a weathered piece of wood he found on one of the beaches they'd anchored at two years ago. Along with their parents, they'd searched for special shells to go with it. That night, the four of them sat around the little kitchen table, gluing shells to the board. It spelled out one word: Family.

"This is Mom's," he said, tucking it under his arm.

Back on the dock, they stood together, taking one last look at a piece of their childhood. Then they turned and walked away, and even though they were tempted, they didn't look back.

Thirteen

Beth spent the next few weeks slowly returning to life. She spent more time with Rachel, Melanie, and Jenny, catching up on the latest gossip and listening to their stories of love. Dylan followed Melanie around like a puppy dog, completely infatuated. And although she never let on to anyone, Beth knew Melanie secretly loved it, and him. Jenny was still dating Brian, and Rachel and Corey were officially in love.

The girls were happy to have their friend back and to see her getting healthy again. It didn't take long for Beth to go back to eating normally, and everything tasted so good. She continued to run, because she loved the way it made her feel inside, and sometimes Jenny and Melanie joined her. Soon, she felt strong enough to surf.

She stood, staring at the waves, realizing how much she'd missed. She'd been in a fog since her dad left and it led her down a dangerous path. He had been livid that they'd left the marina without telling him. Of course, they'd been gone over an hour before he realized it. Beth assumed he was more embarrassed in front of his friends than worried about his kids.

She told him as much after he finished yelling at her on the phone. She hadn't heard from him since. She winced at that. She knew the pain of losing him would always be with her. She hoped it would lessen over time.

"You gonna stand there all day?"

She didn't turn around, she knew that voice. "No, I was waiting for your sorry ass! What took you so long?"

Jeremy smiled. It was good to have her back. He smacked her on the butt and said, "Well, let's go girl!"

They surfed, catching wave after wave. Happy to have them back, the ocean reached up to meet them. It was glorious. When they couldn't take anymore, they collapsed on the beach, exhausted, looking up at the changing colors of the sky.

"It'll be dark soon," he said.

Beth turned onto her side toward him, and he did the same.

"I never thanked you," she said.

"For what?" he asked.

She smiled, and pushed a lock of hair off his forehead.

"For saving me."

He shook his head, "You saved yourself Beth...you saved yourself."

She stared at him for a moment, then said, "I guess I did, didn't I?"

Jeremy nodded, "You did."

He kissed her, and she fell into the sensual abyss he always made her feel, wanting to drown in it. Then she heard a "thump thump thump" in her head. Abruptly, she pulled away.

"Do you hear that?" she asked, hoping he did and that she wasn't hearing things now.

He cocked his head to one side, listening, and nodded.

"It's coming from over there," he said, looking at a group of people that were down the beach a ways. He looked back down at her. "Wanna check it out?"

They put their boards away and walked toward the sound. It progressively got louder and louder the closer they got, until Jeremy said, "It's a drum circle!"

There were about twenty people standing in a circle, and each one had some form of a drum. Some had bongos, some had congas and some had djembes. They were all playing different rhythms with their hands, but somehow, it formed one amazing, pulsating sound. There was a smaller group of people in the center of the circle, dancing.

"Oh my God!" Beth said, realizing one of the dancers was Rachel. Just then, Melanie and Jenny ran up to her. "What are you guys doing here?" she asked.

"Jeremy told us you would be surfing, so we came down to meet you. Then we discovered this!" Jenny said, watching the drummers. "Isn't it awesome?"

Beth nodded. It was awesome. The sound coming from the circle was almost hypnotic. Without realizing it, she began swaying back and forth to the music.

One of the drummers yelled to her, "Go in!"

"Yeah! Let's go in!" Jenny exclaimed.

Beth looked at Melanie, who shrugged her shoulders. "Why not?"

She smiled, and the three girls joined hands, dancing into the circle towards Rachel. She joined her hand with theirs, and the four of them danced around the other dancers. The drumming sped up, and they let go and just danced. Everyone was feeding off of everyone else's energy, to the point where you could almost touch it.

Beth danced her heart out. She danced out the pain, the sadness, the anger, the frustration, the disappointment, the disillusionment. The crowd gave a yell, and she yelled with them. She released her demons, released them to the sky.

Her heart opened, and joy was planted there, and hope. A hope so strong that she was certain of its promise. It promised love.

She looked at Rachel, who had overcome more than any of them and was rewarded with something she'd never known- happiness. At Jenny, who had found acceptance with herself. At Melanie, who finally had the love for which she waited.

She knew that these three girls would always be there for her, just as she would always be there for them. They were her sisters. They would continue to share hopes and dreams, support each other through the rough patches, and always, always celebrate. Celebrate the qualities that made each of them uniquely beautiful.

"I love you," a voice behind her said.

She turned into his arms, knowing that the boy who had been her best friend was now the man she loved. The man who had quietly supported her through the waking nightmare she was finally escaping. He lifted her up in his arms, and she let the music of the drums heal her soul.